A CHRISTMAS CONUNDRUM

STACY WILDER

Cover design by Brandi Doane McCann

ISBN 979-8-9854266-7-0 (paperback)

ISBN 979-8-9854266-8-7 (hardback)

ISBN 979-8-9854266-6-3 (ebook)

www.storystacy.com

Chapter 1

In the background, Bing Crosby crooned "White Christmas." An evergreen candle flickered and released the scent of pine. I opened a velvet lined box and carefully unwrapped the tissue paper protecting the sand dollar shaped glass ornament.

When my new husband returned home from Christmas shopping, I planned to surprise him with a decorated tree. As I gazed at the bauble, memories of our honeymoon surfaced. My eyes scanned the artificial tree branches until I found the perfect spot for the memento that Brad and I'd bought in the Caymans.

As I hummed to the tune, my Labrador retriever, Duke, snored softly by the sofa. A snowy Christmas was unlikely in Charleston and even less likely in Florida where we'd be spending the holidays. My heart fluttered in anticipation of our first holiday with my parents. Duke was startled awake when my neighbor, Lou, burst through the front door.

"Lizzie! *Oh, my gawd.*" He smacked his palm on his forehead. "It's a disaster. What am I going to *do?*"

Duke rushed to greet him, tail wagging. "Hey, boy." Lou patted my dog's head.

"What on earth are you talking about?" Since acting was his hobby, the man had a flare for the dramatic. I was sure whatever was wrong wasn't as bad as his demeanor indicated.

He plopped down on the couch with a grunt. "Someone is *stealing* the Christmas decorations. Last week the custom order for the mayor's big shindig disappeared. And the decorations for Christmas on the Battery are gone. Poof!" He lifted his hands toward the ceiling and flicked his fingers. "And I just had two more employees quit. What am I going to *do*?" he repeated with a distinctive whine.

Lou and my best friend, Peg, had owned an interior decorating firm. After Peg died, Lou'd inherited her share of the partnership. He intended to slowly shift the business from residential design to commercial. However, when Lou and my mom planned my wedding, he'd discovered he had a gift for creating memorable occasions. PeggyLou Designs now offered commercial, residential, and event services.

Since Lou was responsible for decorating some of the most prominent spots in town, I understood why he was so upset. "Do you have any idea who's behind it?"

"I can't imagine who'd be such a Grinch. You *have* to help me find the thief before my *whole* holiday decorating business is destroyed."

Lou and I had been close friends before Peg's death, but we'd become even closer afterward. I was surprised he was just now telling me about the theft. "Have you reported it to the police?"

"I filed a report for the first one, but I wanted to talk to you before going to the cops again." He stared at his clasped hands. "I was hoping my favorite PI might help."

I'd investigated plenty of theft cases, but Brad and I were due to leave for Florida in a week. While I mulled over how I could best assist, my phone rang. I fished the device out of my purse and answered before it went to voice mail. "Mom, can I call you back in a few? Lou's here."

Lou jumped off the sofa and rushed over. "Babs," he shouted as soon as he got close.

He and my mom had become fast friends when they'd collaborated on our wedding. Not many people called Barb, 'Babs.' Lou was one of the exclusive members of the Babs club. My husband had yet to be invited.

"Put her on speaker," Lou said.

I pressed the button and set the phone on an end table.

"Hi, Babs."

"Halloo. How are you?" The pitch of her voice rose a few notches. She sounded more excited to talk to Lou than to me.

"Not good." As he explained his situation, I turned my attention back to the tree.

Lou noted my disinterest and picked up the phone. "I'm going to make a cup of coffee," he mouthed. He took the device off speaker and headed for the kitchen.

As I meticulously placed purple, red, and green glass ornaments equally spaced apart, I wiggled and jiggled to Stevie Wonder's "What Christmas Means to Me."

Duke curled up in his spot by the sofa to resume his nap.

Lou returned from the kitchen with a steaming mug in his hand. "So, it's settled then. Thanks so much, Babs. You're a doll." He handed the phone back to me.

"Honey, I hope you won't mind if we come to Charleston for Christmas," Mom said.

It sounded like a statement, not a question. "Should be fine. Let me talk to Brad and get back to you." I ended the call and glared at Lou. "What just happened?"

He set the cup on the table and grabbed my hands. "Your parents are coming to Charleston for Christmas, and Babs is going to help me with the workload while you solve the crime. Isn't that fantastic?"

"Yeah, fantastic." My voice dripped with sarcasm. My lie-detecting Lab woke up and yipped.

Someone once told me that all dogs have superpowers. Duke's gift was communication. He whined when something was up. He yipped when someone wasn't telling the truth. Very few people knew of his lie-detecting ability, and Lou wasn't one of them.

• • •

As soon as Duke heard the approach of Brad's SUV, he sat by the door that led to the garage. His tail thumped on the tile floor in joyful anticipation.

Brad strode into the kitchen. Multiple bags hung on his arms. He hastily set the packages on the table and gave me a kiss on the cheek before he bent down and lavished love on Duke. "My shopping is done," he proclaimed as he massaged our dog's ears. "I'm all set for Florida."

"Um, about that . . ." I hesitated before continuing.

He stood. "About what?" Duke pawed his leg and begged for more attention.

"How would you feel about my parents coming to Charleston for Christmas instead?" I explained Lou's situation, and how he and my mom had orchestrated the change in plans.

Brad thought for a moment. "Honestly, that'd be great. If we stay here, I can work on the ideas for my next business venture." He whistled the first stanza of "I'll Be Home for Christmas," then added, "Our first married Christmas together . . . It should be in Charleston."

I sighed. My husband was such a guys' guy. It was easy to forget his hidden romantic side. "Thank you. I'll call my parents and let them know. But not until after I show you my surprise."

Brad's brows shot up. "I love your surprises."

I grabbed his hand and pulled him into the living room with Duke in tow.

"Nice job. The tree looks great." He admired my work and then turned and gave me one of those toe-tingling kisses. "Do you think that call to your parents can wait?"

Chapter 2

As I sat in front of the vanity table and applied my make-up, Brad arranged for his private jet to pick up my parents on Monday mid-morning. He set the phone on the nightstand and took a gulp of coffee. "Done."

"If this doesn't get you into the Babs' club, it's hopeless," I joked.

"Not counting on it." He stood and stretched. Our dog hopped off the bed. I was still getting used to him being ours versus mine. Duke and I'd been together for six years before Brad entered the picture.

"See you later, Cougar." He kissed my cheek.

Ever since I'd turned thirty-nine, Brad loved to tease me. I was officially nine months older than him.

"I'll take Duke for a walk and then straighten my office before your parents get here."

At the word "walk," our dog woofed and ran for the door.

"Have fun with Lou." He picked up his coffee mug and followed.

My parents would stay in Peg's old townhome. In her will,

Peg had left Brad the home that was located across the street from mine. It was her effort to play matchmaker from heaven, and it had worked. After our marriage Brad had moved in with me, and he used the townhome as a makeshift office. When he'd sold his identity theft protection company, he tried retiring and then decided it wasn't his style. The walls of Peg's old office were covered with flip-chart paper filled with ideas for his next entrepreneurial venture.

Lou and I were due to meet at Southern Charm, my favorite tea shop, in a half-hour. I had to admit my curiosity was piqued. As I changed into jeans and a turquoise cowl neck sweater that brought out the color of my eyes, I thought about the questions I wanted to ask Lou. I slipped on my boots and then spritzed Amazing Grace on my wrists and neck before I headed out the door.

The breeze was brisk in the near fifty-degree temperature. The humidity seeped into my skin, and I shivered, despite the bright sunshine. Maybe I should have worn my jacket. As I walked, I admired the cherry-red and pastel pink poinsettias perched in window boxes. Joel Roberts Poinsett, a Charleston native, introduced the plants to the states in 1825. An interesting fact I'd learned when I'd played Christmas trivia with my neighbors last year. Streetlamps were adorned with evergreen wreaths and big red bows. The song, "It's Beginning to Look a Lot Like Christmas," hummed in my head.

Ellie, the owner of Southern Charm, greeted me at the entrance of the shop. "Good morning, Liz." She hugged me and then asked, "No Duke?"

"Nah. He's hanging with Brad."

"Lou's waiting for you." She gestured to a booth in the corner. "Hot or iced tea today?"

"Hot, please," I replied before heading to the table.

Lou rose and air-kissed my cheeks. "Doll, you look great. Thanks for meeting me here."

"Were you able to get everything done at your office?" The shop was closed on Sunday, so Lou'd gone in to organize while things were quiet. I slid into the seat across from him and studied the menu. Every time I thought I had it memorized, Ellie changed it up.

"For the most part. I may go back later. I can't wait to see your mom."

Ellie interrupted us with my tea. She set a cup and saucer, a teapot, and a small pitcher of milk on the table. "You two know what you want yet?"

Lou motioned for me to go first.

"What's the special?" I asked.

"Bacon, spinach, tomato frittata, served with fresh sourdough bread."

"Sold." I handed her the menu.

"I'll take the cornbread waffles with hot honey and sausage."

"Got it. You need me to top off your coffee, Lou?"

"I'm good." Lou waited until she was out of earshot. "Here's a copy of the police report with the details from the first theft." He slid the paperwork across the table. "There's no way I'll be able to replace that custom village set in time for the mayor's party. We have to find it. It took the artist months to make."

"When's the party?" I asked as I turned to the page with pictures of the missing items. Wooden replicas of Charleston landmarks were adorned with wreaths and framed with decorated trees.

"Christmas Eve. It's an open house." He sighed. "All the who's who of Charleston will be there."

I did the math. "Ten days from now?"

Lou grimaced and nodded.

I flipped the page to the invoice, and my jaw dropped. The custom artwork had cost fifty grand. "Wow! You have insurance for this?"

"That's not the point. You have no idea how picky the mayor's wife is. We've been planning this since July. Ruth will have a conniption fit if she finds out the village disappeared." He rubbed the back of his neck.

I pulled a notebook and a pen out of my tote. "OK. So, who would want to do something like this? Somebody with a grudge against the mayor? Or someone who's trying to hurt your business?"

"I hadn't thought about it being about the mayor. But that doesn't explain the second theft."

While I waited for him to elaborate, I poured tea into my cup and added a generous helping of milk.

"I ordered over seven thousand dollars' worth of Waterford and Wedgewood ornaments for the Christmas on the Battery celebration at the Edmondston-Alston House. I just reordered and put a rush on it. I'll have to eat *that* expense if insurance doesn't cover it."

"When's the event?"

"This coming Friday. If I'm lucky the decorations will be here Tuesday afternoon."

Ellie arrived with our food. I slipped the police report into my tote and moved my notebook to the side to make room for our breakfast. Ellie topped off Lou's coffee and asked if I needed more tea before leaving us to our food.

Lou buttered his waffles and then ladled hot honey on top. "To answer your earlier question, there are several people who don't want me to succeed."

I tasted a forkful of fluffy egg with maple flavored bacon, spinach, Swiss cheese, and green tomatoes. "Mmm . . . so good." I licked a flake of egg off my lips.

Lou continued, "The owner of Mistletoe Magic is not too happy I've come on the scene. I've taken about fifteen percent of her business away this year, and I'm just getting started." He dropped his fork. "That is, if my reputation isn't ruined after this."

"Any signs she's responsible?"

Lou shook his head and then devoured another mouthful of food. "Oh, my gawd. This sausage patty is to die for. I don't know what herbs she added this time. You have to try a bite." He sliced off a piece and put it on my plate.

"That is good." I savored the flavors before I continued, "What about disgruntled employees or clients?"

"Remember Barbie?"

"Of course." How could I forget Barbie? She'd briefly been on my suspect list in the investigation into Peg's death. When Peg and Lou referred her to another decorator, she was incensed. She'd believed that PeggyLou Designs was her ticket to a feature in *Architectural Digest*. Surely, she still didn't carry a grudge.

"Of course."

"Get this." He waved his fork. "She called and asked if I'd decorate their home for Christmas. She wanted the interior trees decorated with Barbie and Ken ornaments. And a life-sized Barbie car in the yard with Ken dressed as Santa in the driver's seat."

I set my cup back on the table, so I didn't spill my tea. "Get out."

Lou raised his palm. "I couldn't make it up if I tried. Of course, I said no. How tacky."

"No kidding." Knowing Lou, he probably voiced the tacky comment. I jotted Barbie's name in my notebook. "What about your employees?"

"I hired an event coordinator, Sue Ellen. When I interviewed her she seemed qualified, but I've lost a few interns because of her attitude. I can't imagine why she'd want to hurt the business."

I slathered whipped butter onto a piece of sourdough bread. "Any new or ex boyfriends you haven't told me about?"

"Nope. You have the full 411 on my love life."

My brain whirled while I chewed my food. The police report showed that the first theft occurred at a storage facility. "How do you keep track of your inventory?"

"Once we receive an order, we log it into our system. We use the same process for all of the businesses, but there are a lot more items to track for event services. If we have the space, and it makes sense, we store the inventory on site. Otherwise, we move it to our storage facility."

"I assume the unit is locked. Who all has a key?" I took one more bite of buttered bread.

"We keep it on a hook in the copy room. Sometimes the Art Institute interns make a run for us using the company van."

I made another note. "Were the ornaments also taken from the storage site?"

"Yes."

After I inhaled a bite of frittata, I flipped to a new page. "Are you sure all of the items made it to the site?"

His voice rose a notch, and he sat straighter in his seat. "I delivered the village set personally. I turned the place upside down when it went missing, and I've been checking the unit every day since. The ornaments were there, and then they were gone."

Lou sounded confident, and I'd no reason to doubt him. "What's the security like?"

He took a deep breath in and then exhaled. "Cameras, but no guards. I requested the footage from the manager, but I haven't gotten it yet."

"We need to file an official report on the second theft when we finish our breakfast. Do you have pictures of the decorations and the invoice?"

"It's all on my phone." Lou signaled to Ellie for the check. "I got this."

"Thank you." I placed my wallet back in my purse.

"It's the least I can do. And I'm paying you for your time. No arguing."

Although I nodded in agreement, I had no intention of taking money from a friend. When she was alive, Peg had established a foundation that helped the homeless, both people and pets. If Lou persisted, maybe I'd donate what he paid me to the foundation. That would be a good use of the funds. While I packed up my things, I said, "Tomorrow, after my parents arrive, I'll bring Mom to the shop. While I'm there, I'd like to talk to Sue Ellen and your other employees."

Lou reached over and placed his hand on top of mine. "Lizzie, you're a life saver."

•••

As Lou and I marched up the steps to the Charleston police station, I prayed that Lieutenant Sam didn't work on Sundays. Early in my career, I'd solved a few of his cold cases. Sam had never forgiven me. Any lingering hope of a civil relationship had disintegrated when he'd pegged me as the prime suspect in my best friend's murder case.

Lou held the door open for me. A stocky Hispanic female police officer sat behind a glass window framed by a plastic garland and red velvet bows. Boxes overflowing with toys lined the wall to the left. The station's annual toy drive appeared to be going well. I wished I'd thought to bring a donation. Maybe I could write a check or come by another time with a toy.

After we explained our situation, the young woman called for an officer to take the report. Of course, Sam showed up. His bald head glowed in the fluorescent lights, and his bushy brown mustache was dusted with cookie crumbs. Sam was pushing retirement age, and he'd gained a few pounds since the last time that I'd seen him.

"Well, if it ain't Lightweight Liz and her boyfriend Lou. To what do I owe this pleasure?"

I'd earned the nickname when I fainted after hearing my best friend was dead. Interacting with Sam was like listening to fingernails scrape a chalkboard. I wasn't about to waste my breath and explain once again that Lou was not my boyfriend, and I was now married. If Sam was any detective worth his salt, he'd have noticed my ring.

"We're here to report another theft," Lou said.

Sam sighed. "Follow me." He picked up an incident form, poured a cup of coffee into a Styrofoam cup, and led the way down the hall to a familiar conference room. I'd had several meetings with the cops in here during Peg's investigation. I wrinkled my nose at the mildew smell.

Sam didn't bother to offer us anything to drink. "What's been stolen this time?" He clicked the pen and prepared to fill out the form.

When Lou replied, "Christmas ornaments," Sam had the gall to laugh.

"Seven thousand dollars' worth of ornaments," Lou added.

Sam choked on his coffee. "Who the hell pays that kind of money for stuff to put on their tree? You're kidding me, right?"

Lou shook his head. "Trees, as in more than one, . . . and the ornaments are high-end." He located the pictures on his phone and showed Sam.

Sam scratched his jaw. "You got a receipt?"

"Of course. Can I email it to you?"

Sam rattled off an email address. "Send me them pics too."

Thirty minutes later, I had zero confidence Sam would do anything with the information we'd given him. At least Lou had a copy of the police report for the insurance company. And I'd gotten a small genuine smile from Sam when I'd written a five-hundred-dollar check for the toy drive. Of course, he'd made a snide comment that the donation wouldn't influence the priority or the speed of the investigation. *That man.*

"Well, that was a waste of time," Lou commented as we exited the building.

Chapter 3

Brad parked the Rover in the section where his private jet was scheduled to land. While the heat blew from the vents, we waited for my parents' arrival. I took advantage of the extra time and phoned my ex-boss and mentor, Gunner. He owned Bridgepoint Investigations where I'd earned my PI license before I launched out on my own. Maybe he would have a few ideas about how to proceed with the investigation of the thefts. When he volunteered to talk to the manager of the storage unit to get the video footage, I took him up on the offer.

Once the jet landed and then taxied toward us, we stepped out of the vehicle. After a few minutes the door of the airplane opened, and my mom led the way down the steps with a huge grin on her face. My dad towered over her from behind. She embraced Brad first and then me. Dad did the opposite.

Brad grinned. "Barb, Grant. Good to see you."

The porter whisked their luggage into the rear hatch of the SUV.

Mom placed her hand on Brad's arm. "Oh, no, Honey. Call me Babs."

I glanced at Brad and winked.

"Lunch on the plane was divine. The chili and cornbread. And Ben and Jerry's Cherry Garcia. How did you know my favorite ice cream?" She patted her stomach.

"Thanks for the food and the ride," Dad said. Anything that made my mom happy made my dad happy. My heart swelled with love for my family, which now included Brad.

Once we were buckled in our seats, I shared the plans for the day with my parents. "As soon as you guys are settled, Mom and I need to leave for Lou's shop." I turned toward the back while Brad pulled out of the lot. "Lou wants you to get familiar with the store as soon as possible so you can start helping with the events, and I'm going to start digging into the thefts."

"I can't believe someone is stealing from my Lou." Mom frowned. "And Christmas decorations. Who does something like that?"

Brad flipped the radio and "You're a Mean One, Mr. Grinch" poured forth. We all shared a chuckle.

After my parents settled in, my mom and I elected to walk the six blocks to the shop versus driving and trying to locate a parking spot. During the holidays, open parking spaces were impossible to find.

In Charleston, there's North of Broad Street and South of Broad Street. PeggyLou Designs was in an old building South of Broad Street, the chi-chi side. When Peg was alive, the store hours were from ten to three. According to the sign, the shop now closed at five. I'd be able to sleuth for a couple of hours while Mom got acclimated to the business. A buzzer sounded when I opened the door.

Lou emerged from his office and made a beeline for my mom. "Babs!" He embraced her in a bear hug and nearly lifted all one hundred and twenty pounds of her off the floor.

She patted him on the back and kissed his cheek. "Good to see you, my dear."

The receptionist watched their reunion while I scanned the space. Nothing had changed since Peg's death. The walls were still painted chocolate brown. The only difference was an elegantly decorated Christmas tree in the corner and the pink and cream poinsettias on the front desk. Lou had often talked about redecorating. I guess none of us wanted to erase the last evidence of Peg's presence.

As we journeyed down the hall toward Lou's office, I noticed the two rooms reserved for interns were packed four deep, all intent on their computer screens. A woman I didn't recognize was in Peg's old office. The space was stacked with holiday decorations.

"I'll introduce you around in a bit," Lou said. "First, I want to brief you on the business and the upcoming events."

Lou's office was clutter free, and I imagined it was where he met with clients. My mom and I took seats at the polished walnut conference table. A silver vase filled with red and white roses and embellished with holly and greenery sat in the center. Lou picked up a folder from his desk. He handed each of us a sheet of paper with the planned events for the next two weeks. I extracted my notebook out of my tote and prepared to take notes. After I tore a few pages off for my mom, I handed her a pen.

"Who's the woman in Peg's office?" I asked.

"Sue Ellen. She's the new event coordinator." He pulled more papers from the file. "OK ladies, here's a list of all my employees, including the two who recently quit. And copies of their timesheets for the last two weeks."

I was impressed with his preparation. "Do you run background checks on your employees before you hire them?"

Lou looked at me as if I was crazy. "Lizzie, they're students from the Art Institute."

"What about the coordinator?" I persisted.

"Well, no. I've never seen the need to." He removed more documents from the folder. "Here's a list of our holiday inventory.

Presently all accounted for. I had one of the interns do a physical count this morning." He turned toward my mom. "Babs, sweetie, I'd like for you to work directly with Sue Ellen. Maybe you can help me figure out why she's so prickly."

Mom closed her eyes before responding, "I'll try my best."

"Liz, you're welcome to work in here with me, or you can set up in the copy room. Whatever works for you. Any questions before we get started?"

"I'm good. I'm sure I'll have loads of questions later. Mom?"

"I'm OK . . . for now."

"I really appreciate your help." Lou's voice caught. "You have no idea how much this means to me." His ice-blue eyes misted, and he stood to grab a tissue from his desk. After he recovered, we followed him out the door to meet the staff.

After Lou introduced us to both sets of interns, we moved on to Peg's office. Other than the stored decorations, the room hadn't changed. From the diffuser on top of the bookshelf, the smell of magnolia blossoms still drifted through the space. Behind Peg's desk, Sue Ellen was furiously typing on a keyboard.

Lou cleared his throat. "Sue Ellen, I want to introduce you to two dear friends of mine."

She stopped typing and crossed her arms.

"This is Liz Adams O'Connor and her mother, Barb Butler. Liz is a private investigator. She's going to check into the recent thefts."

"Oh, I recognize *you*." She raised her eyebrows. "You were all over the news last year."

Most of Charleston knew me as the PI who'd been accused of her best friend's murder. I could sense my mom's mother-bear hackles as they rose.

"Barb is visiting from Florida. She's volunteered to help us out with the holiday workload," Lou continued. "Before she retired, she was in the event planning business."

Babs's eyes grew wide. Mom used to be an elementary school teacher.

"You should've seen the job she did with Lizzie's wedding," he added.

"Well, I'm glad she's experienced." Sue Ellen rose and shook our hands. "The good Lord knows I don't have the time or patience to train someone. The interns are headache enough."

"Babs, if you're OK, I'll leave you with Sue Ellen. She can fill you in on what's coming up on the schedule."

My mom nodded. The frown on her face didn't match her consent.

"Sue Ellen, I'd like for you to particularly focus on the mayor's party. Arrange for Barb to meet the mayor and his wife as soon as possible. I think Ruth and Babs will hit it off."

Sue Ellen motioned to a chair. "Have a seat, Babs. I'll finish up this email, and then we can get started."

"Please call me Barb."

With those four words, I knew exactly what my mother thought of Sue Ellen.

• • •

As the sun set casting purple and orange hues in the sky, Brad handed the tickets for our tour of the city to the driver. Mom and I climbed into the back seat of the horse-drawn carriage. Brad and my dad sat in front of us. A family of three sat behind the driver. The vehicle was decked for the holidays with garlands and bows; even the chestnut-brown Clydesdale had red ribbons in his mane.

The outing was part enjoyment and part work. I wanted my mother to experience Charleston in her full Christmas glory, so she'd get a feel for what Lou was up against for the mayor's party. As we pulled the provided blankets around our legs to ward off the chill in the air, the horse began to clip-clop down the street.

An instrumental version of "Jingle Bells" played softly from the carriage speakers.

Snippets of my dad and Brad discussing the upcoming college football bowl games carried in the breeze. I loved that the two of them were getting along. Before I asked my mom about her day, I took a moment to admire the baskets filled with greenery and red and gold ornaments hanging from streetlamps.

"It's all so delightful," Mom said. "I'm so glad we came."

"Wait until we get to Rainbow Row and the Battery. You'll love it." I shifted the conversation to the case. "How'd it go with Sue Ellen?"

She rolled her eyes. "She's a piece of work. Don't get me wrong. She's super organized, but I can see why she'd make somebody want to quit."

"What do you mean?"

"She's terrible at giving instructions. Very impatient. And if you get something wrong, well – watch out." Mom sliced her hand across her throat.

"That's troubling."

"What'd you find out, dear?" Mom asked.

"Not much . . . yet. I have a list of questions to ask tomorrow. And I poked through a few of the files in the copy room. It's early."

Mom shivered and clutched the blanket tighter. "I sure hope we can find out who did it soon. Poor Lou."

My mind whirled with potential suspects, one of the staff or maybe the owner of Mistletoe Magic. I shifted my gaze to the street to soak up the sights. Perhaps the scenery would inspire an approach to catch the culprit.

Our guide silenced the music and began telling tales of the Holy City. As he pointed out various churches along the route, he explained that the abundance of churches and a reputation for religious tolerance had likely earned Charleston her nickname.

When we entered the historic area named Rainbow Row, my mom gasped, and everyone became silent. Fresh garlands and wreaths hung from doors, windows, and balconies. The scent of pine was prominent in the breeze.

"This is so much fun," Mom said.

I had to agree. The only thing that would make it more perfect would be a thermos of hot chocolate. I tugged the blanket closer. "Tomorrow before we go back to Lou's, I'm going to run background checks on his employees. I'll let you know what I find out about Sue Ellen."

I was especially interested in Sue Ellen's history. Lou had agreed to let me bring Duke, after I'd claimed my dog helped put people at ease. That was partially true, but not my primary motivation. I wanted to know who was telling the truth, and who was lying.

Once the carriage rounded the corner to the Battery, we all grew quiet as we took in the magical sights. Palm trees and palmettos were covered in white lights. Enormous wreaths made of magnolia leaves hung on wrought-iron fences. Gigantic red bows and massive garlands adorned white columns. Fairy lights and mistletoe decorated arches and gates.

After our ride, we walked to the pub at the Charleston Place Hotel for burgers and drinks. Six-foot statues of nutcrackers greeted us at the entrance. Inside the lobby, lights from towering ten-foot-tall trees glittered across the polished marble floors. Garlands embellished with fruit wound up the dual staircases. The song,"Rockin' Around the Christmas Tree," vibrated in the air.

"I'm impressed," Mom said.

The hotel was one of the accounts Lou had snagged from Mistletoe Magic, and the decorations demonstrated his sense of style. I sighed. Tonight, surrounded by people I loved; I was surely swept up in the spirit of Christmas.

We gathered at the far end of the bar and perused the menus. The bartender took our drink orders, four hot chocolates spiked with Bailey's Irish Cream.

"Oh. I forgot to tell you. Sue Ellen and I are meeting with the mayor and his wife at ten-thirty tomorrow," my mom said.

"Good. The sooner you meet with them the better," I said. "Are you telling her the village set is missing?"

"Not yet. But I am going to try to get Ruth excited about several alternatives."

The server arrived with our drinks. "That was fast," Dad said.

The red mugs were topped with whipped cream and a garnish of rosemary. The sprigs looked like Christmas trees in a mound of snow.

Mom took a sip and licked remnants of cream off her lips. "Anyway, I'm confident you're going to find the culprit and recover the decorations before the party." She set the mug on the bar and patted my leg.

Yikes, no pressure.

Chapter 4

I woke up early to run the background checks and make sense of my notes before heading to Lou's shop. The clock was ticking; it was time to get serious about solving the crime. Duke was curled up in bed by Brad's feet, so I tiptoed out of the bedroom.

After I brewed a cup of tea, I settled into my office upstairs. I logged into my computer and googled Mistletoe Magic. Their website listed Regina Reynolds as the owner. I signed into my background check software and printed reports on each of Lou's employees, Regina, and the mayor. While the printer hummed, I stood, stretched, and then opened the cream-colored paisley drapes that concealed a wall of whiteboard and cork boards. I uncapped a purple marker and wrote "**<u>Suspects</u>**" on the dry erase board. Later, I'd pin index cards and other items of interest on the corkboard.

I grabbed the first batch of reports off the printer, sat in my gray leather chair, and started to read. Regina was divorced and had a couple of kids. Her credit score was shaky, and the cards had high balances. PeggyLou Designs stealing her clients had to sting.

Sue Ellen was married with no kids. Her report was squeaky clean. But wait . . . this was interesting. Regina and Sue Ellen had graduated from the University of Southern Carolina in the same year and were members of the same sorority, Chi Omega. I got up and wrote Regina/Sue Ellen under Suspects and then motive – Money/Save the store. As I sipped my tea, I wondered what Sue Ellen was frantically typing yesterday. Maybe my mom could sneak a peek at her computer.

I picked up the remaining reports off the printer. Ruth was a descendant of the Dalton family. Old Charleston money. Their home had been in the family for centuries. The couple had just celebrated their thirtieth wedding anniversary. They had two grown kids. I remembered reading that they'd been high school sweethearts and had married shortly after college graduation. Ruth's money and connections had funded the mayor's political career. Rawlin Hayes was up for reelection in November of this year. I made a mental note to check out the polls and the other candidates. I imagined the upcoming party was more about campaigning than celebrating the holidays. Although it was unlikely the election factored into the thefts, I wasn't ruling out any possibilities.

Just for grins, I stood and added Barbie to the list of suspects. Motive revenge. She was a long shot for sure, but I couldn't wait to see a Barbie version of Christmas. As I shook my head at the little progress I'd made, Brad entered the room with Duke in tow.

"Good morning, Sweetheart. How's it going?" He kissed my cheek, blew on his coffee, and then took a sip.

I pointed at the short list of suspects. "I have a lot of work to do."

"Hmm." He studied the board. "What about Lou?"

"Lou? Why would he steal his own stuff and then hire me to investigate?' Brad and Lou had gone to high school together and had been friends for years. I was shocked he even mentioned him as a suspect.

"I dunno. Insurance money? Attention?" He hesitated. "Look, I'm not saying he did it. I highly doubt he did, but you're the one who told me you need to consider all the possibilities."

He was right. I uncapped the marker and added Lou, with a motive of money, to the bottom of the list.

•••

Brad dropped me off at Lou's shop along with my mom and Duke. The sun shone in a cloudless sky. Brad was headed out for a day of fishing with my dad on our neighbor Nick's charter boat. Even though there was a chill in the air, the breeze was light, and the water calm; a perfect day to be out on the ocean. Nick's wife, Gwen, was cooking a fresh fish dinner tonight for all of us. My mouth watered in anticipation.

Dressed in a poppy red shift and Tory Burch flats, Mom was all set to meet with the mayor's wife. Before we stepped inside the store, I told her what I'd learned about Sue Ellen. "See if you can snoop into her computer, start with her email."

"I'll try. Maybe I can ask her the usual get-to-know-you questions. Like where did you go to college? See how she responds."

"Good idea." I opened the door.

Duke tugged on his leash and edged past my mom.

"Duke!" She leaned down to brush black fur off her dress.

"Sorry." I said before I headed down the hall. "See you later." I called out over my shoulder while my mother picked off the last few hairs.

"Morning." I said as I entered Lou's office.

He glanced up from the computer he'd been intently studying. Duke pulled me to his desk. He sat and placed a paw on Lou's thigh.

"Hey, boy." Lou scratched Duke's head. "Morning, Lizzie. You two are a breath of fresh air. Where's Babs?"

"With Sue Ellen. Getting ready for the meeting with the mayor and his wife."

He sighed. "This is a nightmare."

"Another theft?" I asked.

"No. The books. My part-time bookkeeper had the flu. She's due to come back tomorrow, but we're so far behind on invoicing..." He patted the stack of envelopes on his desk. "In the meantime, I have all these bills to pay."

"Are you struggling financially? I thought your business was booming."

"It is. And I'm fine for now. It's a matter of cashflow."

Duke didn't yip. "OK. You'd let me know if you needed any money, right?"

"Of course."

At that, Duke yipped.

• • •

After my mom returned from the meeting with the mayor and his wife, we snuck away for a light lunch at Southern Charm. Ellie gave both of us a hug and then slipped Duke a treat. Once we were seated in a corner booth, away from most of the remaining lunch crowd, I quizzed Mom on her day.

"Sue Ellen was so rude. Lou should take her off the mayor's job. It's almost like she was trying to lose the business."

"What'd she do?"

"It's not what she did as much as what she didn't do. She barely acknowledged any of the staff, and her answers to Ruth were clipped. Even condescending."

"That's bothersome."

"I do like Ruth, and I believe the feeling was mutual. She invited the four of us for cocktails tomorrow night. Their home is beautiful. And the decorations are divine. Lou's done such a great job."

"Sounds fun." We'd planned on taking my parents to the Festival of Lights tomorrow night, but it could wait a day.

Ellie placed a water bowl next to Duke. He thumped his tail in gratitude. "Y'all ready to order?"

"What's your soup of the day?" I asked.

"Roasted red pepper, topped with fried green tomatoes."

"I'll take a bowl of that."

"You want your usual iced tea?"

"Yup." I loved Southern Charm's iced tea with a splash of sweet.

"Barb, what can I get for you?" Ellie asked.

"I'll have the same, but regular iced tea for me."

After Ellie walked away, I leaned closer. "Did you get a chance to look at Sue Ellen's computer?"

"Not yet. Maybe I'll have an opportunity this afternoon."

We paused the conversation when Ellie returned with our drinks. I picked up my glass and took a long sip.

"How was your morning?" Mom asked.

Before I could reply, her violet eyes lit up. "Oh my. I forgot to tell you about the hoverer."

"The hoverer?" I repeated.

"The mayor's senior assistant. Wherever we went, he went. Chuck somebody. I can't remember his last name. It was odd."

"Chuck Pickney." I remembered the name from my morning research around the mayor's campaign. He'd been in the position for a year. The mayor's previous assistant died suddenly after a heart attack.

"Yes. That's it. He never smiled once the whole time we were there."

From the pictures I'd seen of him, it appeared that he wore a permanent scowl.

Ellie arrived with our soup, and we were silent for a few minutes as we dipped spoons into the creamy liquid topped with crunchy fried tomatoes. I slipped Duke a piece of bread.

"Delicious." My mom wiped a stray crumb off her mouth with a napkin. "I interrupted you before you could tell me how your morning of sleuthing went."

"I can't say I learned a lot. Most of the staff can't stand Sue Ellen, especially the receptionist, Bernice. But I already knew that. Oh, and Lou's a bit behind on his bookkeeping."

"Poor Lou. So much stress. Maybe I can help him."

That wasn't a bad idea. Lou was more likely to let Babs help than me.

• • •

Back at Lou's shop later that afternoon, I was questioning the intern who'd conducted the most recent physical inventory, when I heard screaming from down the hall.

"What do you think you're doing?" Sue Ellen screeched. "Get away from there. Now!"

Duke whined. We strode toward the noise. I followed Lou into Peg's office where Sue Ellen was yelling at my mom.

"She . . . " She pointed at Barb. "Was snooping on my computer."

Lou put his hand on Sue Ellen's arm. "Please calm down. I'm sure there's a logical explanation." He looked at my mother. "Babs?"

"I'm just trying to learn the business. I thought reviewing the files might help." She shrugged.

Duke yipped.

Sue Ellen sneezed. "What is that dog doing in here? I'm allergic."

Lou ignored her question. "Babs's explanation sounds reasonable to me. Sue Ellen, why don't you join me in my office? You and I have a few things to discuss."

She glared at me before following Lou out the door. "Get your dog out of here."

As soon as they left, I joined Mom behind the computer. She located Sue Ellen's browsing history and discovered her personal email account. Fortunately, she was one of those people who saved their login information. We didn't need a username or password. Sure enough, there were several emails from Regina, the owner of Mistletoe Magic. Footsteps sounded in the hall, so we quickly closed the program, and I took Duke out of the office. I winked at Mom on the way out. "Good work."

As Duke and I were making our way back to the copy room, my phone rang. Gunner's name flashed on the screen. "Hey there. Got anything good for me?" I asked.

"The manager claims he lost the footage. Sorry, kid."

"Well, that sounds suspicious."

"I agree. I got a funny feeling about this."

"What do you mean?" I completely trusted Gunner's instincts. If he had a hunch, I needed to pay attention.

"Didn't like the guy. Can't put my finger on it." He hesitated. "Something about his body language whenever he talked about Lou." Before Gunner hung up, he added, "Be careful."

Lou stopped me in the hallway to let me know that he'd informed Sue Ellen she was off the mayor's account. Instead, he and Babs would handle the details. That news probably went over like a ton of bricks.

Lou told me that he thought it would be better to get my mom out of the office for the day to keep the peace. He wanted Babs to take the van and make a delivery to a client. Since she didn't know Charleston well, he asked that Duke and I tag along and help her navigate the city. The customer lived in the same neighborhood as Barbie. Maybe we'd get a glimpse of her Christmas decorations.

Halfway to the storage unit to pick up the goods, steam rose from the hood of the vehicle, and the check engine light came on. "We need to pull over," I said.

As Mom navigated toward the shoulder, I glanced at the temperature gauge. Not good. I hated to bother Lou with yet another problem, but I didn't know what else to do. He answered on the first ring.

"Lizzie, what's up?" After I explained the situation, he replied, "Impossible. I just had the van serviced."

"Do you have roadside assistance?" I sighed. I dreaded a hike to the nearest gas station.

"Of course. I'll call them right away."

"Thanks." I rattled off our location.

While we waited for help, we listened to Christmas music on the radio. Duke was getting restless in the back. My mom and I sang along to Nat King Cole's "The Christmas Song."

Five songs later, a truck arrived. The technician concluded that there was no leak, but the coolant was low. He topped off the fluids, and we were on our way.

"That could have been a whole lot worse," I said and added, "What if one of the interns had been driving. They probably would've panicked. Somebody could've gotten hurt, and the engine could've suffered a lot of damage."

"Lou needs a new mechanic," Mom said.

Maybe. After my conversation with Gunner, I wondered if someone had messed with the van.

Chapter 5

When we arrived at the storage unit, I took Duke to a grassy area in the back to do his business. My mom went inside to retrieve the outdoor lights and the Nativity scene. I rounded the corner just as she emerged with a panicked look on her face.

"I loaded the lights in the van, but I can't find the Nativity set anywhere."

How could that be? Lou's intern had just checked the inventory this morning, and the Nativity set had been listed as in stock. "Let's search again."

Fifteen minutes later, we were empty handed. Before I called Lou, I wanted to talk to the manager and ask if we could view today's security footage. No way the video could disappear twice.

The office had a single desk and a wall lined with boxes and packing tape available for purchase. "Helloooo," I called out. While I waited, I read a flyer posted on the wall about an upcoming anti-gay seminar at a downtown episcopal church.

A man in his fifties with thinning brown hair emerged from the back. "How can I help you?"

I introduced myself, pulled out my wallet, and showed him my PI card. "Another item's gone missing from unit 22. Any chance I can view your security footage from today?"

"Sorry, cameras went out last night. I can't get anyone in to fix them until next week."

Duke yipped.

I closed my eyes and counted to ten. "Are you positive?" I asked.

He crossed his arms and then nodded.

"Did you see anyone entering or leaving the unit today?"

"Nah, I've been working on paperwork all morning. Other than the random sale of boxes, I've been holed up in my office."

"You have a card in case I have any other questions?" He handed me his business card, and I glanced at it. "Thanks, Alan." Alan Johnson. I'd definitely be checking into his history.

"Have a good day," he said as Duke and I exited the store.

I called Lou to deliver the bad news.

"What . . . Again . . . Are you sure?"

"We looked everywhere. I promise. It's not there."

The line was silent for almost a minute. "You still there?" I dreaded reporting another theft to Sam.

"Yeah, just thinking. Go ahead and drop off the lights. The installers will be there first thing in the morning. I can pick up another Nativity set from Home Depot. I'll deliver it personally."

"OK. I'll stop by the police station in the morning and report it. Maybe I can get an update on the investigation."

"Yeah, right." Lou sounded defeated.

• • •

While the security guard placed a call to the client who lived in Barbie's neighborhood to ensure the delivery was legitimate, I texted Brad.

How's the fishing?

Great! Get ready for fresh redfish.

Yum.

> How's it going with Lou?

OK, but we're running a little behind. We'll walk home and meet you guys at Nick's.

> You sure?

Yep. Could use the walk before dinner.

> K. See you later. Love you.

Love you too. Thanks for hanging out with my dad.

> All cool. Enjoying his company.

We piled back into the van, and after we'd dropped the lights off, we drove by Barbie's house. Sure enough, a life-sized glittery pink car sat in the front yard. In the driver's seat was a plastic Ken doll in a Santa suit. A synthetic Barbie doll in a pink dress with a matching Santa hat occupied the passenger seat. Nine golden retriever statues were hooked to the front of the car. The lead dog's nose had been painted red. I had to admit it was kind of cute.

I asked Mom to park the van on the street. "Let's see if we can get the full tour."

"Do we have time?"

"I already texted Brad and told him we'd be late." We left Duke in the vehicle with the windows partially rolled down. He wasn't happy.

"We'll be a few minutes, boy." I reassured him. I snapped a photo of the Barbie car-sleigh with my cell before we crossed the street.

The front door was flanked by two trees fashioned from pots of pink poinsettias. I rang the doorbell. Barbie's maid, Lydia, answered the door.

"Hi, Lydia. I don't know if you remember me. I'm Liz. I visited Barbie last year."

"Liz." Barbie bounded toward us and edged past Lydia. "Please come in. What brings you here?"

"My mom and I were in the neighborhood, and I was admiring your decorations in the front yard." I turned to my mother, "Barbie, this is Barb."

"Pleased to meet you. Do you two have a few minutes? You *have* to see the house. The decor is dynamite if I do say so myself," she beamed.

"Just a few. We're already late to our next appointment. But I'd love a tour."

"Lydia, bring us some champagne. A tour wouldn't be complete without a glass of bubbly." She winked and motioned for us to follow her into the two-story living room.

Fifteen-foot-tall evergreens were decked out with pink and silver ornaments. Barbie and Ken baubles were spaced between the white lights. It might've been OK, if it weren't for the Barbies dressed in glittery pink dresses at the top of each tree.

"Do you mind if I take a picture?" I asked.

"Not at all."

Of course, she photo-bombed it.

I couldn't wait to show Lou. A fire crackled in the marble fireplace. Fresh garlands embellished with pink ornaments and bows were draped over the mantel. A large pink-and-cream poinsettia sat atop the coffee table.

"Wow," I mouthed as Lydia handed me a flute of champagne.

"Isn't it divine?" Barbie said.

"That's one word for it," Mom said.

I elbowed her, nearly spilling her drink.

"Will you email me the pic?" Barbie asked.

She likely had a huge social following. "Who did the decorating?" I asked.

Barbie flipped a lock of blonde hair behind her shoulder. "Mistletoe Magic." She headed toward the dining room. "Of course, most of the ideas were mine. That friend of yours, Lou, claimed he was too busy to take the job." She took a big sip of champagne. "It all worked out though, I couldn't be happier."

If she carried a grudge, she was a good actress. I mentally crossed Barbie off the suspect list.

• • •

Forty-five minutes later we returned to our townhome community, and my mom went across the street to change. After I fed Duke his premium dog food dinner, I traded my slacks for jeans and pulled a red sweater covered with snowflakes over my head. As soon as Mom returned, the three of us walked next door. Nick insisted I bring Duke. He adored my dog.

When Gwen answered the door, I handed her the bouquet of red roses I'd purchased on the way home. Her glasses were perched on her nose, and she wore her typical cardigan sweater uniform. This one was adorned with gingerbread men. Since Gwen was an elementary school librarian, I was confident she and my mother would have plenty to talk about. A tantalizing aroma of garlic and butter wafted in from the kitchen.

Gwen took the roses and motioned for us to come inside. "Thanks for the flowers. They're beautiful." Duke nudged his way in front of us and made a beeline in the direction of the source of the scent.

"Your tree's lovely," I commented. As we progressed past the flocked tree, I noticed a few ornaments that matched the pictures of the stolen decorations. While investigating Peg's death, I'd discovered Gwen had a habit of shoplifting. Theft would be a whole new level. I hoped I wouldn't be adding her to the list of suspects.

"I finished decorating today. C'mon, the boys are gathered in the kitchen. I'll put these in water, and then we can chat."

"Is that a Wedgewood?" I fingered a blue bauble with a Nativity scene embossed in white on the porcelain surface.

"Yes, I just bought a few new decorations from Mistletoe Magic. Aren't they pretty?'

"They're gorgeous," I breathed a sigh of relief.

Duke sat between Brad and Nick. I sauntered over and gave Brad a kiss on the cheek. "You got some sun." Brad's nose glowed red. He could play Rudolf in a Santa play.

"Nick's a great guide," my dad said. "You won't believe the fish we caught."

By the goofy expression on Dad's face, I could tell they'd all had a few beers.

Nick rose. "Ladies, can I get you a drink? Beer, wine?"

"I'd love a glass of white wine," I replied.

"I'll take a beer," Mom said.

As Gwen placed the roses in a vase, I asked, "So what's Mistletoe Magic like? I've never been."

"Oh, you must go. Bring your mom. It's wonderful and will fill you with the holiday spirit." She fluffed out the leaves of the roses. "But they were short-staffed. Be prepared for a line."

I dipped an oversized shrimp in cocktail sauce and took a bite. "Do you know the owner?"

"Regina? Only from visiting the store. She seemed frazzled this morning."

Barb accepted the beer from Nick. "Gwen, can I help you do anything?"

"Thank you, but no. I've got this. Relax and help yourself to the appetizers."

Gwen had put out quite a spread. In addition to platters of shrimp and crab, she'd made a cute cheeseball shaped like a snowman, and fresh veggies with dip.

After I finished my shrimp, I turned to my husband. "Guess what. Babs snagged us an invitation to the mayor's house."

Brad lifted his beer in a mock toast. "Way to go, Babs."

Mom grinned.

"When?" Dad asked.

I picked up a cracker shaped like a Christmas tree and spread cheese on it. "Cocktails, tomorrow at five."

"Rawlin is a good guy. Y'all will enjoy it," Nick said.

"How do you know the mayor?" Brad asked.

"I've taken him on a few charters. I hope his assistant, Chuck, doesn't join you. He's a piece of work. I was worried a couple of times he was going to chuck our mayor over the side of the boat." Nick grinned at his Chuck joke.

I placed a couple of crab claws on my plate. "Really?"

"Nah. I'm just kidding, but you should have seen the look he gave him when Rawlin wasn't paying attention."

"What do you mean?" I asked.

"Like he hated the guy."

Now that was interesting.

Chapter 6

We left Nick and Gwen's around ten o'clock last night, after a delightful evening of good food and company. Everyone had a belly laugh when we'd told tales about our visit to Barbie World and then shared the pictures.

I was dragging this morning, and I regretted the slice of salted caramel pie I'd consumed after dinner. This morning called for coffee. Once I'd drained the first cup, I poured a second and headed upstairs.

Fueled by caffeine, I started to work. Alan Johnson was a common name, and I didn't have enough information on him to conduct a background search. I tried searching his name and Safe Storage management. That brought up a list of job opportunities. When I googled his name and St. Martin's church, I got a hit. Alan was on the committee organizing the upcoming controversial anti-gay seminar. I clicked on his name on the church website and got a brief bio, including his age and where he'd gone to college.

Would he deliberately sabotage Lou's business because he didn't like Lou's sexuality? But then how would Alan know? Peg had been the one to secure the storage unit before she and Lou became partners. I wondered how long Alan had worked there. After I sent an email to Gunner asking if he could pull additional information on the manager's background, I stood and added Alan to the list of suspects. Motive – Hate.

Since I had an hour and a half before I needed to be at the shop, I descended the stairs and cracked open a few eggs for an omelet. As soon as Duke heard the noise, he joined me in the kitchen. After the bacon, spinach, mushroom, and cheese omelet was cooked, I woke up my husband. "Breakfast is ready." I probably should've invited my parents, but I wanted some time alone with Brad.

"Dang. Smells great."

After I added a forkful of omelet to Duke's bowl, I plated the rest and joined Brad at the table. A few bites in, I asked him if he would do me a favor.

"What'd you have in mind?" he asked before taking another bite.

"Do you mind popping by Mistletoe Magic? Take Duke. If the owner's there ask her a few open-ended questions."

"How will I know who she is?"

I pulled up a picture on my phone. "I'll text the questions to you. I'd go myself, but she'd know something was up."

"OK. Am I getting paid?" he winked.

"Of course." I leaned over and gave him a lingering kiss.

• • •

As Mom and I walked to the shop, she said, "I'm really glad we came here for the holidays. Last night was so delightful."

"Yeah." I patted my belly. "I'll need to spend at least two weeks in the gym to work dinner off." Not to mention this morning's omelet. What was I thinking?

"Relax, dear. The holidays are meant for indulging." As we rounded the corner, she continued, "In addition to visiting the mayor and prepping for events, what sleuthing is on the agenda for today?"

"You're enjoying this." I laughed. "Why don't you see if you can help Lou with his books? I'm curious to know how far behind he is. While you help him out, I'll question Sue Ellen."

"You don't think Lou had anything to do with the thefts?"

"Of course not. Just trying to gather all the facts. And with your knack for numbers, if anyone can sort out his books, you can."

• • •

Sue Ellen and I had a meeting set for eleven this morning. I wished I could've brought Duke to test her honesty, but her alleged dog allergies squashed that hope. I asked the receptionist how Sue Ellen liked her coffee and brought a cup as a peace offering.

"How's my mom handling the work?" I set the mug on her desk.

"Thank you," she smiled.

I'd obviously scored a few points.

"Honestly, she's slowing things down."

If Duke were around, I'm sure he would yip. "Really, how?"

She fumbled with an answer. "Well for one, I have to explain everything to her at least twice."

No way. I fingered the University of South Carolina paperweight atop a pile of papers on the corner of her desk. "I heard you and the owner of Mistletoe Magic went to college together and were sorority sisters."

She choked on her coffee. "Regina?"

I nodded and waited for her to continue.

"We've lost touch, but isn't it interesting that we've ended up in the same business?"

I knew from experience it was too early to jump to conclusions, but Regina and her buddy, Sue Ellen, had risen to the top of my suspect list.

My phone buzzed, and I checked caller ID. Gunner. I glanced at Sue Ellen. "Excuse me, I have to take this." I moved to the hallway to accept the call.

"Hey, kid. I have some info for you." Unlike me, Gunner had good relations and connections with the Charleston police. "I got lucky," he added. "Alan had a traffic ticket for speeding a few months ago."

"That's it?" Surely, he hadn't called just to tell me about a ticket.

"Because of that ticket, I have his birthdate and license number."

I fished my notebook and a pen out of my tote and recorded the details. "Thanks."

"There's more. He was arrested once for protesting at a gay rights rally. But that was years ago."

Interesting. I remembered the flyer in the office when I first met Alan. Before I ended the call, I asked. "What are you doing for Christmas?"

Gunner had lost his wife to cancer several years ago, and he had no kids. "Right now, no plans."

"Join us for Christmas dinner?"

"I'll think about it," he replied.

"We'd love to have you."

After my meeting with Sue Ellen, I strode toward the police station to file the latest theft report. Maybe the walk would work off last night's slice of pie. As I crossed the street, I felt a strange force push me to the side, and a gray Honda whizzed by, nearly hitting me.

"Watch where you're going!" I shouted as the vehicle rounded the corner, spinning away as I strained to catch the license number. No luck. It all happened too quickly. I leaned against a streetlamp while my heart thumped in my chest.

"Are you OK?" A woman with shopping bags draped over her wrists stepped closer. "That car was going way too fast."

"I'm all right," I reassured her. "A little shaken. You didn't happen to see the driver or catch the plate number?"

She shook her head. "Not the number. Just a quick glance at the driver. May have been a white male. Not 100 percent on that."

As my heartrate slowed, I recalled the time in California when an unseen power had pushed me out of the way of danger. In the letter Peg'd left me after her death, she promised to be my guardian angel. If the odd force came from Peg, she was fulfilling her vow.

After I concluded the business at the station, I hurried home. The earlier excitement and the exercise had made me hungry. I hoped to grab a bite to eat and run a background check on Alan before I returned to Lou's shop.

As soon as Brad saw my ashen face he said, "What happened?"

"Where's my dad?"

"He went into town to shop. What happened?" he repeated.

"It's not a big deal. A car came close to hitting me. Startled me. That's all."

"You know you don't have to do this. Even if it is for Lou. It's risky for you, but did you consider the potential risk to your mother?"

OK, that was a low blow. "My mom's a big girl. I don't even know if the near miss was related to the investigation. Besides, we've had this conversation." I crossed my arms. "You know where I stand." We had a long discussion about my profession before we got married. Although I no longer needed the work to pay the bills, resolving a case and bringing a perp to justice was what I did. And it was no accident that a lie-detecting dog had serendipitously entered my life.

The silence in the room was deafening. Duke broke the quiet with a whine.

Brad exhaled and wrapped his arms around me. "I know. But it doesn't mean I have to like it." He kissed my neck. "Hmmm. You smell good. Amazing Grace." Brad loved the perfume I wore with that name.

Amazing grace, indeed.

• • •

I took a bite of my turkey and Swiss sandwich before I logged into my laptop. Duke sat next to me and patiently awaited a stray crumb. I printed the background report on Alan and read while I munched. Alan was a Charleston native. A graduate of the Citadel with a degree in business, he was married with two kids. He was active in his church. Only one arrest record. I set my sandwich on my desk and texted Gunner.

> What was the make and model of the car Alan drove when he got the ticket?

A minute later my phone pinged with a response.

> Gray Honda Accord

Thx

Something was niggling at the back of my mind. I recalled Nick's comment about the mayor's assistant. When I'd researched the mayor and the upcoming election, an article mentioned that Chuck was also a graduate of the Citadel. I located his date of birth and plugged his information into the software. Chuck had graduated the same year as Alan with a degree in Political Science. The Citadel was a military college. The population was around three thousand students, mostly men. I imagined the two had crossed paths. I ran a search on both of their names and Citadel. Turns out they played college tennis together along with the mayor's major contender in the upcoming election, Weldon Barnes.

I was friends with the librarian at the college, Serena. She'd worked there for years. Maybe she could shed some light on the relationship between Alan and the two other men. Duke barked, and I gave him the remnants of my lunch.

Brad hollered up the stairs. "Liz, I'm going to take Duke to

Mistletoe Magic. Will you text me the questions you want me to ask?"

Duke bounded down the steps at the sound of his voice.

"OK." I emerged from my office and blew him a kiss from the top of the stairs.

As I composed a list of questions, I added.

See if you can find out what kind of car she drives.

You got it.

I knew Sue Ellen drove a white Mercedes. If Alan wasn't the driver responsible for the earlier mishap, maybe Regina was the culprit behind the near miss.

Back in my office I stared at my computer and rubbed my chin. Could Chuck or Weldon be a suspect in the thefts? Maybe I needed to find out what kind of cars they drove. I got up and added their names to the suspect list. Motive –? I half-hoped Chuck would join us later for cocktails.

· · ·

As Brad and I got ready for drinks at the mayor's house, he relayed the details of his visit to Mistletoe Magic. Not only had he asked the questions I'd given him, but he'd also improvised and uncovered some interesting information. His detective skills impressed me. Although with his good looks and charm, he could get any woman to spill her secrets.

Brad slipped on his sports coat. "We talked about fraternity life."

He chuckled and told me how he'd pretended he'd gone to the University of South Carolina when he'd actually gone to the other USC, University of Southern California.

"Regina said she was active in her alumni association, and her sisters were big supporters of her shop. I told her Sue Ellen Carter was my former neighbor, and Regina bought it. Claimed the two of them were besties. Duke didn't yip once. Well, except at my lies."

"Were you able to find out what kind of car she drives?"

"There was a gray Honda in the parking lot. I couldn't find an easy way to ask if it was hers without it seeming like a weird question."

"You did good. Thank you."

He picked up a bag off the nightstand and handed it to me. "I bought you something."

I unwrapped the tissue paper to uncover a black Labrador retriever Christmas ornament. "I love it."

"I thought it looked a little like Duke."

"It does." Brad leaned closer, and I stood on my tiptoes and kissed his cheek.

"Is that all I get?"

I wrapped my arms around him and rectified the earlier peck.

• • •

On the way to the mayor's house, Mom filled us in on her efforts to help Lou with the books. "He's two months behind on his invoicing. I was able to catch him up and most of the billing went out."

"Is he going to be OK?" I asked.

"For now." She smoothed the skirt of her black dress. "I'm worried with it being the holiday season. Lou doesn't want to make phone calls, but someone needs to call the clients with the bigger balances due."

"Um, there's something you should know before this goes any further." I hated to add to her worries. "I had a near miss today." After I filled her in, I added, "I'd totally understand if you want to bow out."

Brad glanced in the rearview mirror, I'm sure in an effort to gauge my mother's reaction.

"Honey, I'm so sorry that happened to you." She sat taller. "No way am I quitting."

"Babs . . . don't you at least want to think about it?" Dad asked from his shotgun seat.

Mom glared at the back of his head. "Butlers don't back out."

I smiled. That had been our family motto for years.

After a brief silence Dad said, "All right," then added, "But you girls need to be extra careful."

"Of course," we replied in unison.

Brad held the door open for me as I climbed out of the Rover. "You look great," he said.

"Thanks. So do you." Both my dad and Brad wore rust-colored chinos and navy blazers. I'd chosen a flowing emerald-green silk shirt and black pants. Since I'd never been to cocktails at a politician's home, I hoped I had dressed appropriately.

We strolled up the steps of the sprawling three-story Victorian style home. Cream-colored fabric roses and magnolias adorned an enormous garland over the entryway. Gold ribbon garnished with glitter twined around the greenery. Oversized boxwood wreaths with golden bows and gold-glittered ornaments hung on the dual dark green wooden doors. Ruth opened the door before we had a chance to ring the bell.

"Babs, thank you for coming." Ruth smiled brightly at my mom and gestured for us to step inside. "This must be your lovely family."

After Mom made the introductions, we followed Ruth to the living room. The mayor and Chuck rose from the sofa. "What are y'all drinking?" Rawlin asked after the handshakes were done.

As we gave him our orders, the mayor began to fix the drinks. While I waited for my wine, I admired the huge tree. The magnolia topper nearly touched the ceiling. Pink lights twinkled amongst ornaments featuring various Charleston landmarks. "Your tree is beautiful, Ruth."

"Thank you." She handed me a glass of chardonnay. "Everything is going to be so perfect for the party."

I glanced at my mom as she grimaced.

"I've really enjoyed working with Lou on this project and getting his view on the state's gay rights issues," Rawlin said.

It was common knowledge that the mayor was working with our governor to pass a law prohibiting discrimination based on sexual orientation or gender identity. "It'll be an uphill battle to get the new law passed. But I'm confident once I'm elected, we'll get it done. After all, the LGBTQ community is a growing part of our state's population. Don't you agree, Chuck?"

Of course, it was all about the vote. Chuck looked up from his phone. "Yeah. If anyone can help the governor make it happen, it's my man, Rawlin." His face was expressionless.

Brad accepted his glass of scotch from Ruth and took a sip. "That legislation is long overdue. I'm glad you're tackling the issue, Mr. Hayes."

"Oh, no. Call me Rawlin. Y'all are coming to the party, right?" the mayor asked.

"Of course. Wouldn't miss it for the world. Thank you," Mom said.

Chuck scowled, "Yeah, it'll be *the* Christmas party."

Ruth frowned. "Ladies, join me outside? Babs, I have an idea I want to share with you." As soon as we were out of earshot, she said, "I swear sometimes I don't know if Chuck is really behind my husband." She held the back door open, and we stepped onto the porch.

"What do you mean?" I asked.

Ruth sighed, "Last week, Rawlin missed a lunch meeting with a major donor. Chuck swore he told him about it, but it wasn't on his calendar." She wiped the condensation off her glass with a napkin. "I'm sure it was an honest mistake. I tend to get the jitters around campaign time."

"Is Chuck always so . . . surly?" my mom asked.

Ruth laughed, "Pretty much. But enough about Chuck. Let's talk about the party. What do you think about having Santa for the kids? We could put him in the gazebo."

I could sense the wheels turning in Mom's head as she visualized the surrounding decor. "Great idea, Ruth. It'll be a big hit, even with the adults."

"The weather forecast is promising, and my brother's agreed to play the part. My daughter-in-law can take pictures," Ruth added.

"Good. It's settled then," Mom said. "I'll start working on the design tomorrow and run it by you."

Ruth smiled. "Thank you. It's a lovely evening, why don't I ask the boys to join us outside?"

The temperatures had cooled to the low fifties, and the breeze was light.

Minutes later Ruth returned with a tray of bruschetta, crab-stuffed mushrooms, pickled vegetables, and spinach dip. Rawlin placed a stack of plates and napkins on the table along with a basket of sour dough bread. He handed out cigars to the guys. "Ladies?"

My mom and I declined.

"Please, help yourselves to the food and then take a seat." Ruth motioned toward the east end of the deck. "We'll want to sit up wind from the cigar smoke."

I picked up one of the porcelain plates. After selecting a few crab-stuffed mushrooms and pickled carrots, I spooned a generous dollop of spinach dip onto the dish. Once I'd confirmed the breeze was blowing in the right direction, I sat in the rocking chair closest to the guys and perched the plate on my lap. Chuck was in the seat next to me.

"I understand you're a graduate of the Citadel," I said.

Before he replied, he lit up his cigar and took a puff. "Yep."

"My friend, Serena is the librarian. She's been there forever. Do you remember her?"

"Name's familiar."

Getting the man to talk was impossible. "She refuses to retire. She loves her job." I sunk my teeth into a mushroom as I contemplated how to word my next question. The juice dribbled out the side of my mouth, and I wiped it away with a napkin. "Isn't the mayor's main contender also a Citadel alum?"

"Yeah. We used to be friends. Played on the tennis team together. But we lost touch."

I wished Duke was with me. "You don't happen to know Alan Johnson? He was probably there when you were. Business major."

Chuck wrinkled his nose and a crease formed between his eyebrows. "Pretty common name. Doesn't ring a bell."

Since Alan was also on the tennis team, I'm pretty sure my dog would've yipped at that statement.

Chapter 7

First thing the next morning, I placed a call to my favorite librarian.

"Liz, it's wonderful to hear from you. How are you?"

"Great, but I'm way behind on my Christmas shopping."

"I'm almost done. Grandkids are easy, but I doubt you're calling to chat about the holidays. What's going on?"

Serena had assisted me with research in the past. My calls were rarely social. "Well, I *could* use your help on something."

"As long as it's not buying gifts, name it."

I filled her in on the current investigation and asked if she remembered Alan, Weldon, and Chuck.

"Sure do. Thick as thieves, those three, and very ambitious, especially Weldon." She paused. "By the way, Weldon's speaking today at a fundraising luncheon. If you'd like to meet him, I can snag an extra ticket. Want to be my guest?"

"I'd love to." I could sleuth and hang out with my friend.

After we worked out the details, I called my mom.

"Good morning, sweetheart."

"I enjoyed last night. I hope you and Ruth keep in touch."

"Me, too."

"There's been a slight change in plans. I'll drop you off at Lou's, and then I'm going to run surveillance on Alan. Afterward, I'm attending a luncheon where the mayor's contender is the keynote speaker. I may try to observe Regina for a bit after that."

"Oooh, surveillance sounds like fun."

"Trust me. Most of the time, it's boring." Thanks to my thoughtful husband, I now had a Sprinter van equipped with the latest detective gear. It even had a bathroom.

"OK. Between prepping for the upcoming events and catching up on Lou's financials, my day is full anyway."

"You guys still want to tour the Festival of Lights later?" I was amazed at my parents' energy at their age. I hoped it was genetic.

"Can't wait. So far, Christmas in Charleston has been wonderful."

I said a silent prayer that the wonderful trend would continue. If anything happened to my mother, it would be my fault and the guilt would plague me forever.

• • •

I changed into a long-sleeved black shirt and pants. Before I left, I inspected the van. It was well-stocked with water and snacks. My black baseball cap and sunglasses were tucked inside the console. I plugged my phone into the provided charger and drove to Alan's home in North Charleston. I parked down the street and waited.

A few minutes later, a Honda backed out of the garage. I picked up the binoculars on the passenger seat and peered through to ensure Alan was behind the wheel. Once I'd confirmed it was him, I turned on the ignition and followed him, staying several cars back.

Alan turned into a shopping center and stopped in front of the pharmacy. Fifteen minutes later, he emerged carrying a bag that sported the store's logo. I continued the tail, keeping a safe distance between our vehicles. After a mile, he signaled and made a right turn into an older neighborhood. A few blocks in, he pulled into a driveway and got out of his car. A woman with snow-white hair rose slowly from a wicker chair on the front porch and embraced him in a bear hug. I switched on the audio amplifier from inside the van and listened in on the conversation.

"Morning, Mama. Here's your medicine." He handed her the bag. "How are you doing?"

"I'll be better once I solve this dang crossword puzzle. What's a six-letter word for private investigator? Starts with a S."

"Sleuth?"

"That's it. My smart boy." She sat in her chair and penned the answer. "How are the boys?"

"Good. Winter break starts tomorrow."

"Y'all sure I can't bring anything for Christmas dinner?"

"Just you." He looked at his phone. "Listen, Mama. I need to get to work."

"Of course, you do. My smart boy," she repeated. "You still picking me up for church on Sunday?"

"I'll be here." He leaned down and kissed her cheek. "You take care of yourself, Mama. Don't forget to take your medication."

When we were back on the highway, I expected Alan to take the exit for the storage facility, but instead he drove toward downtown. He stopped in front of a townhome in a neighborhood a few blocks from the Citadel campus. I parked, flipped on the audio equipment, and zoomed in with my camera.

After Alan knocked, the front door cracked open, and someone handed him an envelope. Alan opened the flap and extracted a bundle of money. He discreetly counted the cash before he returned to his vehicle. Once I'd snapped a few pictures and jotted down the house number, I followed him to his next destination, the storage facility.

While I waited across the street for Alan to make his next move, I googled the address of the townhome. It belonged to Chuck Pickney. Seems like Chuck knew Alan after all. I glanced at the time. Thirty minutes to get home, change clothes, and exchange the van for my Volvo. I was going to be late to the luncheon.

• • •

As predicted, I arrived at the Citadel ten minutes late. I scanned the crowd and found my friend. After I greeted Serena, I slid into the seat next to her. "Thanks for inviting me."

"My pleasure." She introduced me to the other folks at the table and then asked, "What's my favorite sleuth reading?"

"Sue Grafton's *Q is for Quarry*,"

"That's a good one. Have you read Patricia Cornwell's latest? Highly recommend."

"No, I'll have to check it out."

While the Citadel president introduced the speaker, a server placed plates of chicken salad in front of us.

I glanced around the room. There were ten tables of five. The ticket price must've been hefty. When the president concluded his introduction with, "Please hold your questions for Mr. Barnes until after his speech," I began mentally preparing my list.

Once the thirty-minute drone on about nothing was finished, I raised my hand.

Mr. Barnes gestured my way. "Yes, young lady at table two."

An assistant brought a portable microphone. I stood and started with an easy one. "What was it like playing on the Citadel tennis team?" Before sitting, I added, "And do you still play?"

Weldon grinned a fake politician grin, showing off his snow-white teeth. "Our team was very competitive. Taught me a lot about life and running a campaign. We all keep in contact. Some of my teammates are my biggest backers. Unfortunately, I don't have as much time for tennis anymore, but I do still play." He scanned the crowd. "Next question?"

After ample time for others to ask questions, I raised my hand. "How do you feel about the governor's proposed new legislation prohibiting discrimination based on sexual orientation or gender identity?"

"Excellent question. I'm one hundred percent opposed to it. As my daddy used to say, if it ain't broke, don't fix it. Just imagine all the money lawyers would make if that passed."

A small chuckle reverberated through the room. I wasn't sure how what I'd learned factored into the missing Christmas decorations. But I did know one thing without a doubt. Chuck most definitely kept in touch with his old Citadel friends.

After the luncheon, I stopped by the house to exchange my dress for jeans and a Charleston hoodie. I pulled my hair back in a short ponytail and threaded it through a baseball cap. With dark sunglasses, I hoped I looked like any other tourist. I slipped my earbud amplifying device into my purse and headed for Mistletoe Magic. Time to check out Regina for myself.

When I entered the store, I spotted Sue Ellen and Regina in an animated conversation by the gift bags. I lowered my cap, slid the earbud in my ear, and took position out of sight behind a Christmas tree.

"I'm sorry. He took me off the account," Sue Ellen said.

I strained to catch the words that got lost amid the overhead music in the store.

Regina replied. "I need the account back. And the other ones he's stolen from me."

"I don't know how—"

"I don't care how. Just do something."

Sue Ellen fished around in her oversized satchel and retrieved a piece of paper. "Here's a copy of his pricing. Maybe you can undercut him?"

Regina snatched the price list. "I'll do whatever it takes."

"Liz!" my neighbor, Cassie, called out. "Fancy meeting you here." I put a finger to my lips and hustled out the door. I bet Cassie would come calling later to find out what that was all about. In the meantime, I hoped that Sue Ellen and Regina hadn't spotted me.

• • •

In the evening my parents, Brad, and I strolled through the Festival of Lights. Since the night was clear with a slight breeze, we'd elected to take the walking tour versus driving at a snail's pace through the park. Duke led the way, tugging on the leash Brad held in one hand. We'd bundled up in coats, hats, and scarves.

We arrived at the Dancing Lights display and stopped to watch. Instrumental Christmas music played while trees adorned with colored lights flashed on and off to the rhythm of the music. Duke made friends with a nearby golden retriever, nuzzling, and wagging his tail.

Then the lights went out, and the music stopped.

The audience fell silent, and a slow buzz of conversation started as everyone speculated about what had just happened. Spots of light began appearing like fireflies as people used their phones as flashlights. Part of the crowd rushed out of the area. Duke whined and then growled. I heard my mother grunt as she fell to the ground. Someone in a hoodie grabbed my hand and shoved a piece of paper into it.

"Mom, are you OK?" I called out.

"I'm fine." We all gathered around the source of the sound. Dad bent and grabbed her elbow to help her stand. "Somebody pushed me. Probably one of the people who got spooked and panicked." She brushed grass off her coat.

After what seemed like an eternity, but was likely only a few minutes, the lights came back on. I held the note by the edges and unfolded it.

Stop investIgating NoW OR SOMEthing wOrSE Might HAPPEN to your MOM.

The letters used to make the crude message had been cut out of a magazine and glued on to the page.

"What's that?" my dad asked.

I read the note out loud.

"Let me see," Brad said.

"No. The fewer people who touch it the better. Even though it's a long shot, I'll dust it when we get back to the house. Maybe I'll get lucky."

"It's high time you girls stopped these shenanigans. It's just Christmas decorations," Dad said in the tone he used when I was in trouble.

"I'm with Grant," Brad added.

I glanced at my mother. "Maybe they're right."

She straightened her spine and crossed her arms. "What part of 'I'm fine' did you not hear, Grant? This isn't just about the decorations. Lou's business is at stake. Butlers don't back out." By the look on Mom's face, I knew she'd just doubled down.

Chapter 8

Brad woke me up early. "I'm going for a long bike ride, and then hitting the gym. Can you walk Duke?"

My husband's triathlon training continued despite the weather. His next race was in Colorado this spring. "Sure."

He pecked my cheek. Although he hadn't said a word, I imagined he wasn't happy that I'd decided to continue with the investigation. Nightmares of something awful happening to my parents had caused a restless night with little sleep. I rolled over hoping to catch a few more ZZs, but Duke had heard the word walk and was pawing the side of the bed.

"OK, boy. I'm up."

After he'd howled the words "I love you" for his breakfast, I took my tea upstairs and packed my tote. Last night, I'd dusted the paper for prints and had discovered only my marks at the edges where I'd gripped the note. The person who created the document had most likely worn gloves. I recalled the texture of leather when the note was forced into my hand.

Once I'd taken pictures of my white board, I whistled for Duke and braved the cold for the ten blocks to my office. I needed a change of perspective.

The old red-brick building north of Broad on King Street was in the non-chi-chi side of Charleston. Six workspaces of varying sizes occupied the second floor. The first floor contained a gift shop. Most of the time, I worked from home, but occasionally I needed space to meet a client, or like today simply a change of scenery.

No one else was crazy enough to be here at six a.m. on the Friday before Christmas. I exhaled, and a misty cloud of breath danced in front of me. The place was freezing. I kicked the thermostat a few notches up and then unhooked Duke from his leash.

My office, the smallest one on the floor, had enough space for a desk, an ergonomically correct chair, a couple of chairs for clients, and a dog bed for Duke. Centered on the polished pine door was my name on a removable brass plate. Inside, the only artwork was a framed copy of my PI license. One wall was exposed red brick; the other was painted with special paint so I could use it as a whiteboard. Most of the tenants had glass fronts to make up for not having a window. Instead, I had a wall covered with cork to pin index cards, pictures, and whatever else might visually help with a case.

Still in my coat and gloves, I unpacked my bag while Duke curled up in his bed in the corner. If someone was threatening my mother, whoever was taking the decorations believed we were getting closer. I recreated my notes on the whiteboard in this office and then started making a list of questions. Who knew Babs was my mom? Most of the suspects, other than Alan. Was somebody stealing the decorations for their own use? A long shot but I hadn't considered the possibility. Maybe we needed to install our own security cameras inside the storage unit to see if we could catch the culprit. And why was Chuck giving Alan wads of cash?

Frustrated, I plopped in my chair and tried to recall the details of the previous night. The person who'd handed me the note had been dressed in a black hoodie and black pants. From the little I'd been able to make out, he or she was slim, maybe around five foot eight. None of the suspects on the list matched the height, but Regina's oldest boy was a freshman in high school. Could it have been him? It'd be awfully low to put your kid up to pushing an old woman, but Regina had sounded pretty desperate.

What had either Babs or I done to make someone so rattled? Was it my visit to Mistletoe Magic? Had either of the women spotted me?

I stood and added the dates the thefts were detected. The first two had been discovered early in the morning. I lasered in on the latest incident. It had occurred between Tuesday morning and early Tuesday afternoon. Sue Ellen and Lou had been at the office. I remembered Gwen had seen Regina at Mistletoe Magic on Tuesday. That left Alan and Chuck as possibilities.

Deep in thought, I jumped when my phone pinged with a text from Brad. How was it already almost eight o'clock?

Where are you?

I typed a quick reply.

At my office downtown.

Seconds later I received another message from Brad.

Lou's here. There's been another theft. Your mom and dad are on the way over.

How bad?

Bad.

My heart dropped.

Oh no : (On my way.

When I arrived home, Lou had already explained the situation to my parents, so he had to repeat the whole story.

"All the Christmas decorations?" I asked in disbelief.

"Everything except a wooden Grinch yard statue," he replied as he paced our living room.

I filled Lou in on Sue Ellen's betrayal.

"Doesn't matter, I'm finished. There's no way I'll recover." His shoulders slumped.

"We can help," Mom said. "What's missing?"

Lou handed her a long list. "This is the latest report of the all the Christmas items that were in storage. I checked the unit yesterday. It's accurate."

After Mom studied it, she handed the document to me. "Lou, we got this. Five of your clients paid you via ACH yesterday. You have the cash, and I know how to shop. We don't have to buy all the stuff at once. Your first delivery today isn't until three o'clock. Between the five of us we can divide and conquer and get it done."

It was no wonder my mother had commanded an elementary school classroom for years. Babs was in her full take-charge mode.

"Liz and Brad, fetch your laptops. We'll find where we can buy this stuff and put together a plan."

"Yes, ma'am," my husband replied. "Why don't I get my flip chart paper from across the street, and we can map it all out?"

"Good idea," Babs replied.

Lou wiped a tear away from the corner of his eye. "Y'all are the best."

An hour later, we had a course of action. Mom and Dad would hit the Target, TJ Maxx, and Home Depot south of Charleston. Brad and Lou would canvas the spots north of town. I'd file a report with the cops and get a camera installed inside the storage unit. We'd reconvene at two p.m. before the delivery to the first client. Between all of us, we should be able to cover the deliveries through

Sunday. Since I'd be otherwise occupied, at least the person who'd given me last night's note would believe we were taking heed.

The neighborhood Christmas party was at Cassie's tonight. I wished we could beg off, but I'd have to come up with a creative excuse to dodge the get-together. I reminded the team we needed to be ready to attend the gathering by seven o'clock.

"I'm not sure I'm up to it," Lou said.

"If you don't go, Cassie will never forgive you. Besides it'll be fun. Lord knows we could all use a break," I replied.

• • •

We arrived at Cassie's at half past seven. I handed Cassie the Christmas cactus I'd picked up after installing the camera and filing the police report. Of course, Sam had been working. Lou and Babs had successfully made the three o'clock delivery. We were set through the weekend. Despite the adrenaline that still coursed through my veins, I hoped I could relax. We joined the rest of the neighbors in the living room. Cassie had put Nick in charge of making the drinks.

The tree was tucked in the corner by the fireplace. A tin star topped the fir. Red plaid ribbon wove between the branches. Faux candles flickered. A matching plaid tree skirt was piled high with gifts.

"Thank you for the cactus," Cassie placed it on the coffee table. "And what was the shush to the lips at Mistletoe Magic?"

At sixty-plus, Cassie was still sharp as a tack and not afraid to ask questions.

"I didn't want them to know I was there. It's part of an investigation." I tried to keep my response as brief as possible.

"Are they involved in the thefts from Lou?"

Of course, Cassie already knew what was going on. "Too early to tell." I sniffed the air. "What's cooking? Smells good."

"Spinach casserole, baked oysters, quail bites, and garlic infused scallops."

Yum. The one dish that would make the meal better was lobster.

"Oh, and did I mention lobster claws?"

I licked my lips.

"Did you remember your gift for the white elephant?" Last year's gift exchange had been a blast. My stomach hurt at the memory of the belly laughs.

"Of course." I extracted four small packages from my oversized purse and set them under the tree. "What game are we playing?"

"Christmas bingo."

"Sounds festive."

After dinner, we gathered around the tree. Cassie handed out bingo cards and explained the rules. Each square contained a question about the holidays. Whoever answered the questions correctly in a line, and then called out bingo would win. The winner would have the last steal in the white elephant swap. Everyone else would take their turn according to the number at the top of their card.

Cassie gave us the go, and I started filling in my answers. I'd nearly forgotten about Lou's troubles until I saw the question about the movie, *How the Grinch Stole Christmas*.

Chapter 9

While Duke ate his breakfast, Brad drank coffee, and I sipped my tea. "Last night was fun." I commented.

"Yeah, I think your parents enjoyed themselves."

I'd won bingo and had stolen a bottle of Peppermint Mocha Kahlua from my neighbor, Linda. Since she'd wound up with a set of Christmas potholders that were likely Gwen's contribution, she wasn't happy. When this mess was settled, I'd have her over for a drink to make up for the steal. Babs had ended up with a pair of elf slippers. Dad had snagged a Santa hat that lit up and played, "Santa Claus is Comin' to Town." Brad scored a pair of reindeer socks.

My cell phone lit up. After I answered, I put it in speaker mode. "Morning, Mom."

"Come join us for breakfast. I made snowman pancakes."

I rolled my eyes. I swear sometimes she thought her only child was still six, but I still smiled. "Be right over."

"Lou's coming too." She sounded awfully cheery for seven in the morning with a full day in front of her.

Ten minutes later, we were seated at the table. As my mom set plates of snowman-shaped pancakes in front of us, she smiled. "I had a dream last night. We were all celebrating because the case was solved in time for the mayor's party."

"Mom, it was a dream." I stabbed a snowman in the belly with my fork.

"I know, but I have a really good feeling about this."

I glanced at Lou. Dark bags hung under his eyes. He was uncharacteristically quiet as he picked up a piece of bacon from the platter in the center of the table.

"Any chance your dream identified the thief?" I asked.

"No. But you're going to figure that part out," Babs replied as she took her seat.

• • •

"You're in a mood," Brad said as we walked home.

"What if I don't solve the case? . . . What if Lou's business is ruined? . . . What if something happens to my mom? . . . It will all be my fault," I lamented as the Catholic guilt monster whispered in my ear. My mentor, Gunner's words popped into my head next. "The guilt trip isn't worth your time. Focus on finding the perp."

Since I was expecting Brad to encourage me to drop the case, I was surprised when he said, "Your mother's right. You're going to solve the crime."

I stopped in my tracks. "Thanks."

"I mean it." He turned around and kissed me. "Any chance I can improve that mood before you set out for the day?"

Of course, I said "Yes."

• • •

After we made love, I left Brad to walk Duke. My legs felt like jelly, and the tension in my neck had eased. Brad and my dad had plans to do nothing. I was envious. My plans were to file the report for the latest theft and then run surveillance on Sue Ellen and Chuck. Since Sue Ellen claimed she had family in town and had taken the weekend off, I was curious to find out if she was telling the truth. Mom and Lou would be setting up three parties for clients.

This evening would be a lot more enjoyable. As soon as Lou'd heard my parents were confirmed for Christmas, he'd bought tickets at the local theater to treat us all to tonight's show, *A Miracle on 34th Street*. Last year, he'd played one of the lead roles but had bowed out this year due to the Christmas workload. The five of us would meet up later for dinner before the musical.

• • •

Sam drummed his fingers on his desk as he reviewed the list of stolen goods. "You sure your boyfriend, Lou, ain't staging the thefts for the insurance money?"

"He's not my boyfriend. And, yes, I'm positive." My earlier improvement in mood evaporated. "Can you please fill out the report?"

"Sure thing, Lightweight Liz. You're awfully cranky. You want a donut?" He passed a box of powdered sugar concoctions my way. Maybe even Sam had gotten in the Christmas spirit.

"Thanks, but no thanks."

Thirty minutes later, he'd completed the form and consumed two donuts. He passed it over for me to sign and date.

"Who's working the case?" I asked.

"A new kid, Chance. A real go-getter. Don't worry, if your boyfriend did it, he'll figure it out."

As I exited the station, the Butler in me kicked in. I was determined to solve the case before Sam decided Lou had stolen his own inventory.

• • •

Parked close to Sue Ellen's home by nine a.m., I waited. From two houses away, I admired her perfectly manicured lawn. A collection of gold reindeer was scattered strategically throughout the yard. Someone had already turned off the lights wrapped around the magnolia trees. I didn't see any extra cars, but maybe the alleged relatives had flown in. At nine-thirty sharp, a gray Honda pulled in front. I flipped on the audio amplifier, as Regina climbed out of the car.

Sue Ellen opened the front door. "Good morning. Let me grab my coat then I'll be ready to go."

Sue Ellen appeared a few minutes later decked in a tan Burberry trench coat. While they hastened down the sidewalk, Regina said, "Thanks for helping. We have five parties today including a kid's party. I was supposed to set some of this up yesterday, but between being short of supplies and staff, it didn't happen."

After they drove away from the curb, I waited a minute before tailing them. Their first stop was Mistletoe Magic. Regina traded the Honda for the company van, and the women began loading the vehicle with the supplies for the parties. I spotted a few items identical to the missing inventory. But the decorations were common and could've been purchased in any store. There was no way to tell if the pieces were the stolen goods.

Once the van was loaded, I followed them to a home in West Ashley. Regina set a helium tank behind the vehicle and started blowing up balloons. She handed Sue Ellen a few shaped like Christmas trees, and Sue Ellen tied them to the mailbox. When the balloons were finished, they filled a rolling cart with party goods. Regina set the tank back in the van and closed the doors.

A woman opened the front door of the home, and two young girls bubbling with excitement for the upcoming party bounded outside. After the chaos calmed, everyone returned to the house, out of range of the amplifier. The van's windows were tinted. I'd have no luck if I tried to peek in and locate any possible stolen goods while Regina and Sue Ellen were otherwise occupied. So, I waited.

An hour later, they were back on the road.

I was beginning to think following them was a complete waste of time until they stopped at the second house in a nearby neighborhood and unloaded a few items I recognized; two nutcrackers meant to flank a fireplace and a set of glittery gold Christmas trees in varying sizes. Was it just coincidental that the decorations matched the ones missing from Lou's storage? I followed my instincts and snapped several pictures. I'd confront Sue Ellen with the evidence later. For now, I had what I needed.

Before moving on to check out Chuck's house, I fueled up with a peppermint latte and a shortbread cookie from my favorite bakery, Sugar Bakeshop. After I'd parked down the street from the townhome, I turned on the audio amplifier. As I munched on the cookie and sipped my coffee, a white Mercedes sedan backed out of the home's garage. Chuck emerged from the house and waved at the car. The vehicle stopped, and the driver rolled down the window. Chuck walked over, leaned inside, and kissed what I assumed was his wife on the cheek. "Have fun shopping." He whistled a lively tune I didn't recognize as he headed back to the house.

I zoomed in with my high-powered camera lens and searched the windows for activity. The wooden blinds were raised, and Chuck entered the kitchen. As he pulled items out of the refrigerator and cabinets, I wondered what he was up to. He didn't strike me as a cook or baker. He set four large Tupperware pitchers on the counter and put a stockpot on the stove. Chuck cracked eggs over a bowl separating the whites from the yolks and then blended in sugar. When he poured cream and milk into the saucepan, I concluded he was making eggnog. After he sprinkled nutmeg over the pan, he grabbed a blue plastic bottle and shook it before mixing the contents into the concoction. I zoomed in closer. Why was he adding Milk of Magnesia? I attempted to snap a few pictures. A good quality shot from this distance was unlikely, but it was worth a try.

• • •

I needed to ruminate on what I'd learned before taking any further steps. I stopped by my office downtown and added notes to the whiteboard. I'd made some progress, and I was leaning toward Sue Ellen and Regina as the culprits. But there were still too many loose ends and no strong evidence to tie any of the suspects to the crime. While the question about Alan accepting cash from Chuck glared at me like a neon light, the next steps in the investigation began to take shape.

Tomorrow, after Mass, I'd confront Alan at his mother's house and threaten to tell her *all* about his nefarious dealings *unless* he tells the truth about the missing items and the mysterious cash. Hopefully the bluff would work, and I'd glean new information. Next, I'd visit Sue Ellen and question her about the venture with Regina on Saturday. As a last resort, I'd show Chuck the grainy picture I took and ask him why he was spiking eggnog with a laxative. I was desperate and determined to solve the case.

Was I on the right track? I called Gunner and shared my plans.

"Facing down suspects sounds risky, kid," he said after I'd outlined the details. "Take somebody else with you. I'd come, but I promised my sister I'd join her tomorrow for an early holiday celebration." Gunner's sister lived in Columbia, a two-hour drive away.

"OK. Glad you're getting back out. What'd you decide about Christmas dinner?"

"I'll be there. You're right. It's been long enough."

"Excellent."

Chapter 10

Over dinner last night, we'd all worked out the details of my plans. After Mass, Mom and I would take the Sprinter to Alan's mother's house. My dad and Brad would walk home. We'd wait for Alan to finish Sunday lunch with his mom and then confront him. Afterward the two of us would pay a visit to Sue Ellen. On the way to Chuck's, we'd pick up my dad and Brad for reinforcement. Lou would have to be on his own for deliveries tomorrow.

I hoped our tactics would force someone's hand.

While I'd watched last night's play, I'd prayed for our own Christmas miracle. We needed it.

• • •

Dressed in our Sunday finery, we slid into the pew three rows from the back. I wasn't taking any chances if Father Joe went overtime on the homily. The priest and deacon wore the traditional vestments. Sunlight filtered through stained glass windows casting prisms of light onto flocked trees. As the heater blew, the advent candles flickered.

"I love this church," Mom whispered in my ear.

Unlike me, Babs rarely missed Mass. If I was a good Catholic, I'd skip communion. I was way overdue for what they now called the Sacrament of Reconciliation. The church held a mix of memories for me. It was where Peg's funeral Mass had taken place and where Brad and I'd been married. As the service began, Brad squeezed my hand.

When the first notes to my favorite Christmas hymn, "Oh, Come All Ye Faithful," started on the organ, I took it as a sign. We were getting closer. I could feel it. Although the God I understood was forgiving, He also had a passion for justice.

• • •

My mom and I waited in the Sprinter for Alan to emerge. After thirty minutes, he exited the front door and waved goodbye to his mother.

"Mom, hurry." I called out to Babs, who was making use of the convenient bathroom. "He's leaving." I pocketed the pistol I kept in the glove compartment and jumped out of the van. We'd parked right behind his car by the curb. I positioned myself in front of his driver's door and turned on the small recording device in my pocket.

Mom climbed out of the van and blocked the passenger side.

Alan strode over to where I prevented access into his car. "What the hell?"

I placed my hands on my hips. "Exactly. *What the hell* were you doing at Chuck Pickney's house a few days ago? Looked like you were getting a huge wad of cash." I showed him the picture on my camera.

"So. I don't have to tell you anything. Get out of my way." He attempted to push past me.

"Hate to tell your mama what you've been up to," I said.

"Yeah, don't break your mother's heart," Mom added.

I grimaced. We'd agreed I'd do all the talking.

"It'll break her heart either way. You tell her. Or she finds out when I go to jail." Beads of sweat formed on his forehead.

Jail? I quickly formulated a response. "Tell you what. You help me, I help you. I can get a deal for you. Keep you out of prison."

While a plea bargain wasn't a guarantee, between Gunner's relationships, my mother's connection to the mayor, and Peg's family's influence, I had some leverage.

"How do I know you're not bluffing?"

"Your choice. I march in there now and tell her everything I know. Or you take a chance I can help you."

I could almost see the wheels spinning in his head. After several long minutes, his shoulders slumped, and he said, "OK."

Turns out Chuck and Weldon had a grand scheme to derail the mayor's campaign. Stealing the decorations to embarrass the mayor was a small piece of it. Alan had agreed to participate out of loyalty to his tennis mates and the chance to put a gay out of business. The money was a bonus. The stolen decorations were in a separate storage unit onsite.

"Get in your car and drive us to the unit." I pulled the Ruger out of my coat pocket and pointed it at him. "Mom, in the car. Back seat."

Babs' eyes were wide as saucers. As Alan drove, I kept the gun pointed at the back of his head and barked instructions at my mom. "Let Brad and Dad know that our plans have changed, and they need to meet us at the police station. Then call Ruth and put her on speaker." I handed her my phone and told her the pass code. "Find Liam in my contacts and call him after that."

After Mom contacted Ruth, she pressed the speaker button. Ruth put her phone on speaker as well, so her husband could hear the news. The mayor was devastated to learn that Chuck was planning his downfall. He promised to speak to the police chief about Alan's bit part in the whole ordeal.

After we ended the call, Mom phoned Liam. I felt horrible I was just now reaching out to Liam and Camille, Peg's parents. I'd been meaning to phone weeks ago . . . their second Christmas without Peg.

When Liam answered, I apologized for not touching base sooner.

"It's good to hear from you. There's no need to apologize. How are you doing?"

I explained my current dilemma. "I need your help."

"On it."

I promised to visit them after the holidays were over.

On the way to the storage site, Alan expanded on the plans to take down the mayor. They included missed appointments, rumors leaked to the press, and schemes to enrage the mayor's largest donors. In exchange for disrupting the mayor's campaign, Weldon had not only promised Chuck the deputy-mayor position, he'd also promised to appoint him as the head of the Community Development Advisory Board where Chuck would be able to obtain inside information on future real estate deals. Graft, a form of political corruption resulting in personal gain, was a serious federal crime.

Alan's thefts paled in comparison.

Peg's brother, Ian, was an attorney. If Alan cooperated and helped put Weldon and Chuck behind bars, between Liam's connections and Ian's expertise, I felt comfortable a deal could be negotiated.

After Alan unlocked the storage unit where the stolen decorations were housed, I put the phone on speaker and called Lou. The entire hand-painted custom village leaned against the far wall, intact. "We found the stolen goods. Babs and I solved the case." I snapped a quick picture and sent it to him. "The mayor's party is saved."

A few moments of silence passed. I imagined that Lou was trying to compose himself. "I knew you two could do it. Thank you, Lizzie. Give Babs a kiss."

Alan frowned, as a big grin spread across my mom's face.

We delivered Alan to the police station. My dad and Brad had already explained our discovery to the police chief. Since the allegations against Chuck and Weldon were federal offenses, a couple of local FBI agents greeted us when we arrived. Of course, Sam immediately took credit for solving the case.

Thanks to Liam and Rawlin's efforts with the police chief and the Feds, if Alan cooperated, he wouldn't serve jail time for the thefts. Although he'd be on probation for a while, the sentence would likely be less than a year. As a personal penance, he offered to waive Lou's rental fees for the next three years.

Later that afternoon Chuck and Weldon were arrested and turned over to the FBI. Chuck confessed that he'd agreed to help Weldon for the promised positions. Weldon was less cooperative.

On the drive to the police station, Alan had revealed that Chuck had planned to take the laxative-laced eggnog to the mayor's party. When I shared that tidbit with Brad and my dad, Dad said, "Well, that'd be a party pooper." We all doubled over in laughter.

The four of us left to pick up the van we'd parked in front of Alan's mother's house. I'd drive the van home. Did Chuck's wife know about the tainted eggnog in her fridge? Since I didn't want her to get sick, I took a side trip to Chuck's house.

She nearly shut the door in my face. "You're the PI who just put my husband in jail."

Well, I think he did that himself. I was only the PI who ratted him out. "I thought you might want to know that the eggnog you have in your refrigerator is contaminated."

"I hate eggnog." She slammed the door with a resounding boom.

* * *

Christmas was almost here, and I had yet to shop. While Mom and Lou staged the decorations for the mayor's Christmas Eve party, I combed downtown Charleston for gifts. At my favorite bookstore, I purchased a boxed set of mystery novels for my mom, a montage of thrillers for my dad, a nice pen for Lou, and a leather journal for Gunner. The best part was they wrapped the gifts for me. One less thing on my to do list. I popped into Sugar Bakeshop and bought tins of cookies for my neighbors. At the pet store, I stocked up on rawhides, toys, and treats for Duke's stocking and contemplated what to get Brad. Struck with inspiration, I nearly skipped to the next spot.

• • •

On Christmas Eve, Brad and I sat in the rockers on Rawlin's back porch. Kids and adults formed a line across the spacious yard to sit in Santa's lap. The queue for the outdoor bar was just as long.

"It really is a miracle," I said. "Everything's perfect."

"I knew you'd solve the case."

Lou sauntered over. "Can I join you?"

"Of course."

"Doll, I can't thank you and Babs enough. I'm indebted for life."

"I can't believe Alan targeted you just because you're gay," I said.

Lou replied, "It wasn't the first, and it won't be the last time that happens."

"That's just wrong," Brad said.

Lou fidgeted with his cocktail napkin. "At least I'm getting free rent. Makes up for some of the extra inventory I had to order."

"That was an awfully nice thing you did for Regina," I added. After Lou and my mom had set up the party, he'd gone by Mistletoe Magic and asked Regina if she'd like to collaborate with him for next year's celebration.

"There's plenty of work to go around. I can't let a single mom struggle like that." He took a sip of Christmas punch. "Sue Ellen turned in her resignation. Too bad Babs can't move here permanently."

My parents joined us, taking the seats next to Lou.

"The village turned out wonderful. That will be a family keepsake for decades." My mom patted Lou's hand. "I'm going to miss you, my friend."

"You'll have to come back soon. I'll be a mess without you. Thank you, Babs."

"You'll be fine, dear," she responded.

• • •

On Christmas morning we opened our gifts, sipped on hot spiced tea, and munched on Mom's famous coffee cake. Brad loved the cargo bike I bought him so he could cycle Duke around the city. He gifted me a beautiful blue opal and diamond pendant necklace. The colors reminded me of the ocean. In the afternoon, we feasted on turkey, stuffing, mashed potatoes, green beans, salad, and pecan pie.

And just like that Christmas was over. My parents were headed home tomorrow. I knew I'd be devoting next week to the gym.

• • •

As Dad rolled their luggage up to the back of the Rover for the trip to the airport, Lou joined us to say goodbye.

"Bye, Babs." Lou hugged my mom. He wiped a tear off his cheek before helping my dad load the bags into the SUV.

Mom's eyes misted. "Bye, Dear. Next year you'll have to come to Florida for Christmas."

"I'd love that."

Mom winked. "Get Brad to give you a ride on his jet."

Seriously, were Lou and my mom already orchestrating next year's holiday plans?

While Mom climbed into the car next to our dog, Dad held the opposite door open, and I took my seat on the other side of Duke. Before he closed the door to take his shotgun seat, he leaned in and said in that dad tone, "Liz, I hope you'll stop this investigation business. And soon. It's too dangerous."

"I'll think about it."

Duke yipped.

Acknowledgments

My mission is to deliver a good read to the reader and benefit a larger community. A portion of the proceeds from this book is donated to Feeding America and other organizations that help the homeless. A big thank you to my readers, I couldn't exist without you. If you enjoyed the story, I would sincerely appreciate a rating or review.

It indeed takes a village to create a book. A big thank you to my beta readers, Mary Ellen, Tim, Gloria, Tricia, Robert, Christine, and Karen. Many thanks to all who supported me along the way, most especially my greatest cheerleader, my husband. Thank you also to my parents, my Aquafit helpers, my author and artist friends, my Charleston friends, my cover designer, and my editors.

Keep turning the page for Liz's recipes and a sample from the first book in the Liz Adams Mystery Series, *Charleston Conundrum*.

All the best,
Stacy Wilder

Bab's Famous Sour Cream Coffee Cake
Serves 10-12

Cream together with a mixer:

1/4 cup butter, softened

1 cup sugar

2 eggs

Slowly mix in:

2 cups flour

1 teaspoon baking powder

1 teaspoon baking soda

Blend in:

1/2 pint sour cream (1 cup) – *tip use a little extra for a moister cake*

1 teaspoon vanilla extract

Preheat oven to 360 degrees.

Pour + one third of the batter into a well-greased Bundt pan (enough to cover the bottom of the pan). Separately melt 3 tablespoons of butter. In another bowl, combine 3 tablespoons of sugar and 3 tablespoons of ground cinnamon. Sprinkle half of the cinnamon mixture on top of the batter, then add the remaining batter. Pour the melted butter on top and sprinkle the remaining cinnamon mixture. Bake at 360 degrees for thirty-two minutes or until a cake tester comes out clean. Allow to cool for fifteen minutes before inverting the pan to release the cake. Delicious warm with a pat of butter.

Peg's Percolator Spiced Tea
Serves 10-12

Ingredients:
2 ½ cups unsweetened pineapple juice
2 cups unsweetened cranberry juice
1/4 teaspoon salt
1 ¼ cups water
1 tablespoon whole cloves
3 sticks cinnamon
1/3 cup brown sugar

Pour juices and water into the percolator. Place remaining ingredients in the basket and perk. Serve hot. If you don't have a percolator, you can use a saucepan. To modify for a saucepan, add the brown sugar, salt, and cinnamon sticks to the liquid. Place the cloves in a loose tea basket and bring to a boil. To turn it into a cocktail, add a splash of golden or orange rum to each mug. Garnish with a cinnamon stick.

The Christmas Conundrum Playlist:

1. "White Christmas," Bing Crosby
2. "What Christmas Means to Me," Stevie Wonder
3. "It's Beginning to Look a Lot Like Christmas," Bing Crosby
4. "I'll Be Home for Christmas," Bing Crosby
5. "You're A Mean One, Mr. Grinch," Thurl Ravenscroft
6. "Jingle Bells - Instrumental," Elvis
7. "Rockin' Around the Christmas Tree," Brenda Lee
8. "The Christmas Song," Nat King Cole
9. "Winter Wonderland," Johnny Mathis
10. "Santa Claus Is Comin' to Town," Bruce Springsteen
11. "Oh, Come All Ye Faithful," Perry Como
12. "O Little Town of Bethlehem," Aaron Neville

Prologue

Liz stretched the packing tape over the last box. The movers were due to arrive any minute. Referring to the yellow legal pad, she double-checked her list.

"Stock options cashed—check. Divorce papers finalized with lying, cheating bastard of an ex-husband—check. Atlanta house sold—check. Closed on townhouse in Charleston —check. Signed up for classes to obtain PI license—check." A tear escaped from the corner of her eye. "Damn it, Sawyer," she swore at her ex.

She chewed on the end of her pen and looked around the boxed-up space they once called home. The hardwood floors lovingly restored. The walls painted a soft cream. They'd spent hours picking out the perfect shade. The upstairs bedrooms would never be filled with the children they both had so desperately wanted. Thirty-one and divorced. Not the life she'd imagined a few years ago when she believed in their love. His betrayal still stung. Her blue eyes misted. "No more tears." She brushed off her hands in an attempt to dismiss any lingering memories.

A wet nose nudged her leg. "Hey, Duke." The puppy was a last-minute addition to the trip. One of her co-workers at Coca-Cola couldn't keep him. At six months, he was already fifty pounds of boundless energy. Who could resist an adorable black Lab puppy?

"Dog crate ready for road trip to Charleston—check."

Her cell phone buzzed, and she recognized the number. "Hi, Mom."

"Hi, hon. You all packed?"

"Yup."

"Are you sure you want to go? Why don't you come to Florida and spend a few months with Dad and me?"

Liz swallowed hard as tears threatened once again. "Too late. Movers will be here any minute. I'll call you when I get there."

Her parents were convinced she was having a nervous break-down after the divorce. They couldn't believe she quit her cush job, sold the house, and was moving to Charleston, South Carolina.

"Suck it up," she muttered. Then she perched her petite frame on the built-in window seat and watched for the moving van. She didn't think it was possible to fall in love with a place, but Charleston gave her hope she hadn't felt in a long while. Time for a fresh start. As she tucked a stray blonde hair behind her ear, she recalled the moment she decided to move.

Walking down East Bay, her whole life upended, a soft salty breeze offered some relief from the sweltering heat. She could feel Charleston seeping into her skin. It was as if nothing mattered and everything mattered all in the same breath. The slight scent of hay and horse sweat coming from a nearby carriage beckoned her to rest her feet and take a ride. Facing a pending divorce and a career that kept her busy, yet not satisfied, she was not looking forward to returning to Atlanta. This place enchanted her. Homes, hundreds of years old, were painted the colors of Crayola crayons. The never-ending Southern porches were dotted with wooden swings and wicker rockers. The azalea and camellia bushes were in full bloom and the scent of jasmine collided with the salt air. The clip-clop rhythm of horses' hooves against the weathered street left her longing for a more natural rhythm in her own life. Every one of her senses was engaged; the backs of her thighs sticky with sweat against the hard brown leather carriage seat; the smell of salt, hay, and perspiration; the Caribbean green, periwinkle blue, carnation pink of the houses; the taste of salt as she licked her dry lips; the musical sound of birds singing. She sighed. It had been a long time since she had felt this alive. Perhaps it was time for a permanent change of scenery.

The sound of the moving van approaching her driveway popped her back to the present. Planting a kiss on top of Duke's head, she said, "Charleston, here we come!"

Chapter 1

SIX YEARS LATER

Duke's baritone bark rang in my ears. Sirens screeched. I jerked upright. The neon lights on my bedside clock pulsed four fifty-two. Heart hammering, I emerged from the warm cocoon of blankets atop my four-poster bed. The jolt of cold tile on my feet lifted a portion of the fog created by last night's third glass of wine.

"What's the matter, boy?" Red lights beaconed through the front bay windows. My sixth sense kicked in, and the hairs on my arm responded. I grabbed Duke's leather collar and edged past his ninety-pound muscled body to peer through the beveled glass of my front door.

My stomach dropped. Police cars swarmed my neighbor's house.

My neighbor, Peg, and I had become fast friends shortly after I moved here. Just six hours ago, we'd polished off her stash of merlot. The good stuff … that she'd bought at a charity auction … for three times the normal price.

I couldn't imagine why every emergency crew in Charleston was parked in front of her home. I ran my fingers through my hair in disbelief. "What the hell is going on?"

After slipping into my robe, I left Duke inside and marched toward the red lights and swarm of emergency personnel. Each step felt heavy and leaden. My gut clenched tighter and tighter, and I wiped beads of perspiration off the back of my neck. The yellow tape stretched across the sidewalk leading to her front door screamed "crime scene." Streetlamps glowed in the morning mist, and the combination of pulsating red and orange lights gave off an eerie glow. Neighbors trickled from their homes and formed a small crowd. I scanned the faces but couldn't find Peg. Picking up the pace, I headed toward Cassie, the sixty-year-old widow, who lived next door to Peg.

"Cassie, what happened? Where's Peg?"

"I don't know." She shook her head.

My legs trembled, and I had a sinking feeling in my stomach. "What happened?" I repeated. "Why are the cops here?"

"I don't know." Her voice rose a few decibels. "Last night I thought I heard a loud pop, like a firecracker, but I'm not sure. I fell asleep with the television on. Went to the kitchen for a glass of water. Turned off the television and crawled back in bed. The next thing I heard was the sirens."

"What time was that?" The most likely neighbors to have any information were Cassie and Lou, Peg's other neighbor and business partner. Peg and Lou owned an interior design firm.

"Around two," she replied.

I'm not popular with most of the Charleston police force, and that was an understatement. I challenged their good ole' boy club. Even though I owned a Labrador, I operated more like a bulldog. What most of them resented, second to my track record, was my ability to navigate through the Charleston elite. I relied on Peg's friends and connections often.

I dreaded trying to drag information out of the cops.

Matt walked up, adjusting his holster. The ginger-colored-cowlick he sported on top of his head made him look like he'd just rolled out of bed. Matt was one of the few members of the Charleston police force who was actually friendly toward me. Peg had nicknamed him Howdy Doody.

 "Howdy, Liz."

"What happened, Matt? Where's Peg?"

Matt gazed at the ground. "I'm sorry, Liz. She's dead."

That was the last thing I remembered before my world went black.

When I opened my eyes, two EMTs were hovering over me. I had no idea how long I was out. With assistance, I stood, my legs wobbling. The EMTs escorted me to Lou's house, insisting that I lie down on his couch. After checking my vitals, they finally left me alone. My head throbbed. I couldn't believe I'd fainted. It must have been the combination of adrenaline and last night's alcohol. Jeez, I dreaded the ribbing I was bound to receive.

I glanced around Lou's living room and into the dining room. Matt and another cop were seated at the glass dining room table, interviewing my neighbors. Cassie fussed over me with a thick soft cotton washcloth dipped in ice water. She'd appointed herself my official caretaker. Brushing her hand away, I sat up, pulling the blanket tightly around me. I was chilled to the bone even though it was likely eighty degrees outside. The month of May was proving itself hotter than normal.

"How long was I out?"

"Not long. Less than a minute," Cassie responded.

"Is she really dead?" This wasn't happening.

"I'm sorry, Liz. It's true."

"Not Peg." I shook my head in disbelief. She was only thirty-six. She would be thirty-seven in July. Our birthdays were nine months apart to the day.

Lou sat on my other side and draped his arm around me. I turned toward him, staring into his long-lashed blue eyes. "How did she die?" Tears rolled down my cheeks. Aware of the cops looking my way, I gratefully accepted the handful of Kleenex from Cassie, blew my nose, and attempted to compose myself.

Lou rubbed his face with his palms. "Bruce found her. He had the early shift at the hospital and was walking Buddy before work." He paused.

Bruce, a divorced doctor, lived two doors down from me.

Sighing, Lou continued, "Peg's door was wide open. He called for her. When she didn't answer, he went in. He found her laying in a pool of blood. He couldn't help her. She was already gone. The cops said she was shot."

"Murdered?"

Lou nodded.

Shivering, I gripped the blanket tighter in an attempt to get warmer and hide my robe. Nausea surged. I leaned back on the couch and closed my eyes.

"Honey, you seem awfully pale." Lou placed his hand on my thigh. "You're not going to faint on us again, are you?"

When I didn't reply, he motioned for Cassie. "Will you bring Liz a cup of coffee laced with brandy? The brandy's right next to the coffee pot."

A few minutes later, Cassie handed me a steaming mug of coffee, and a plate filled with various types of melon, and a croissant. "You need to eat."

I inhaled the smell of the freshly brewed coffee before tasting it. The caffeine seemed to settle my stomach. I mouthed a thank you, noticing that she remembered to salt the fruit for me. After a few sips of coffee, I ate a couple of pieces of honeydew melon and nibbled on the croissant.

Matt motioned that it was my turn to be questioned. Setting the plate of half-eaten food on the coffee table, I stood, still feeling a bit wobbly. I took a deep breath, attempting to pull myself together as I walked toward the dining room.

Sam, a crusty old cop who resented me for having solved two of his cold cases, snickered. "Have a seat, *Lightweight Liz.*" I grimaced as both cops chuckled, and I prayed the new nickname didn't stick. I wanted to punch back with a snarky comment, but I bit my tongue.

Sam glowered at me from the head of the table. His bald head reflected the light from the chandelier. His bushy brown mustache needed a trim. "Where were you last night?"

"At Peg's house."

Matt and Sam glanced at each other in surprise before Sam continued, "What time was that?" Matt flipped to a new page in his notebook and started to take notes.

"Around seven. Her ex, Alex, had called earlier. She was upset."

Sam rolled his eyes. "About what?"

"He asked her for money to cover his debts. She usually caved, but this time she didn't budge." Leaning forward, I slapped the table. "He threatened to kill her."

"Calm down, Liz." Matt chided.

I pulled the blanket tight over my robe. "Don't tell me to calm down, Matt."

He nodded. "Sorry. Continue."

"Not much else to tell. She hung up on him. She was pretty shook up."

"He ever threatened her before?" Sam resumed control of the questioning.

"He has a temper. He was violent at least once while they were married that I know about. Peg told me it was bad enough that she had bruises. He's not a good drinker."

"What time did you leave?" Sam asked.

"Around ten?" I didn't know why I said that when it was more like midnight, but I didn't correct myself.

"Anything else we should know?"

"I didn't like the situation, so I gave her my old Rossi 38 Special. I told her that I'd had it repaired but I hadn't had a chance to take it to the range to test it. The safety tended to slip," I explained.

Matt pushed back in his chair.

"Go on," Sam said.

"Peg assured me she could handle the weapon. She promised to return it as soon as she purchased a gun of her own and asked me for advice on what type she should get." I gazed at Matt and then Sam. "Why didn't she use it to defend herself?" I asked, incredulous.

"No comment," Sam quickly said before Matt could answer. He handed me a grubby business card. "Call if you think of anything else. And Liz, if you keep fainting, you might want to give up the PI business."

"No chance, Sam."

"Fine. Just remember—this is *my* investigation."